I0825200

MOTHMAN IS MY BOYFRIEND

TEN TALES OF CRYPTID LOVE AND LUST

McKAYLA COYLE

For my friends
I wrote this book for you
I hope you can see yourselves in it

Library of Congress Cataloging-in-Publication Data
Names: Coyle, McKayla author
Title: Mothman is my boyfriend : ten tales of cryptid love and lust / McKayla Coyle.
Description: Philadelphia : Quirk Books, 2026. | Summary: "A collection of short stories set in the town of Cryptid Creek, featuring romances with creatures such as Mothman, the Loveland Frog, and Sasquatch"—Provided by publisher.
Identifiers: LCCN 2025037525 (print) | LCCN 2025037526 (ebook) | ISBN 9781683695189 hardcover | ISBN 9781683695196 ebook
Subjects: LCGFT: Monster fiction | Romance fiction | Short stories
Classification: LCC PS3603.O965 M68 2026 (print) | LCC PS3603.O965 (ebook) | DDC 813/6–dc23/eng/20250825
LC record available at https://lccn.loc.gov/2025037525
LC ebook record available at https://lccn.loc.gov/2025037526

ISBN: 978-1-68369-518-9
Printed in China
Typeset in Alkaline, Dapifer, and Hawlers Two
Designed by Paige Graff
Cover and interior illustrations by Wendy Stephens
Production management by Mandy Sampson

Quirk Books
215 Church Street
Philadelphia, PA 19106
quirkbooks.com

Quirk Books' authorized representative in the EU for product safety and compliance is Easy Access System Europe, Mustamäe tee 50, 10621 Tallinn, Estonia, gpsr.requests@easproject.com.

10 9 8 7 6 5 4 3 2 1

CONTENTS

CRYPTID CREEK
BOTANICAL GARDEN
LUCY AND CLEO
BOOK STORE
BOOKWRAITH
JAVALOPE
COFFEE SHOP
CANDY
SHOPPING DISTRICT
THRIFT
THEO
KOREAN B-B-Q
GROCERIES
SANDWICHES
KARAOKE
SCREAMIN' DEMON
THE AVENUE
FLATWOODS
CLINIC +
FIRE DEPT
THAI FOOD
GRIFFIN
JUNE
THE NEIGHBORHOOD
LOVELAND
NESSIE
LILLIAN

SHOPPING DISTRICT

THE AVENUE

THE NEIGHBORHOOD

Prologue

WELCOME TO CRYPTID CREEK

The forests of the Pacific Northwest are mysterious places. Dense, dark, and misty, full of sounds and strange animals. Sometimes the woods feel like they might go on forever. Bird calls echo for too long, footsteps are too muffled. All that can be seen of the sky is a somber gray peering through the treetops. Everything is alive, everything seems to be watching. The moss, the lichen, the bushes full of shining berries, the spindly flowers that grow low to the ground. The trees most of all. The map quickly becomes useless. The compass spins and spins.

It's been two days in the woods and you're starting to worry that you'll never get home. This was supposed to be an easy hike. The guidebook promised it would take a few hours at most. Panic is setting in. There's no way to know where you've been, no way to know where you're going.

Then you hear it. The sound of running water. Faint, but not far off. Hurrying through the trees, tripping on roots and rotting stumps, you move toward the sound. Finally, a break in the trees. A creek flowing over polished rocks, green and brown and blue. Strands of algae wave in the water, tiny fish dart with the current. Moss grows in thick tufts on the bank. Without hesitating, you follow the water upstream.

A wisp of blue sky peeks through the clouds. There's something up ahead. It's an old wooden footbridge, soft with age. A good sign. Someone was here once. Maybe someone still is.

You follow the gentle curve of the creek until you hear something through the trees. Laughter, people talking. You run into the woods, toward the source of the sound. After a few yards, you stumble into a clearing. The sun breaks through the clouds overhead. You're in a small town. A town you don't remember seeing on your map.

Tired, hungry, covered in dirt, you stagger to the street. Almost immediately, someone stops to ask if you're all right. You look up to reply, but find yourself unable to speak. The being before you is not a human. He's several feet taller than you. His body is covered in a thick layer of salt-and-pepper fur. His feet are enormous. Somehow, though, the most surprising thing about him is that he's wearing a flannel and jeans. He puts a large hand on your shoulder.

"Where'd you come from?" he asks. But you can't answer. Your vision is fading to black, your thoughts scattering.

When you wake up, you're sitting on a wrought-iron bench, the handsome bigfoot at your side. He hands you half a baguette and a bottle of water. You accept gratefully. The bigfoot tells you that what happened to you is common. Most people have a hard time adjusting to the Creek for the first day or so. You ask: Adjusting to the Creek?

"Cryptid Creek," he says. "That's where you are. It's strange place, but it's a good place." He tells you he's going to show you around. What is there to do but follow the bigfoot?

The street is busy with foot traffic. There are humans like you, but there are also many other creatures. The bigfoot points out different beings and tells you what they're called. The white blobs with two long legs are nightcrawlers. The doglike individuals with spines down their backs are chupacabras. There are so many more. But you're surprised by how calm you feel. All of this seems—if not predictable, then somehow expected. Like in the most base, most instinctive part of your brain, you knew a place like this must exist.

The bigfoot takes you past a coffee shop, a movie theater, several restaurants. There's a plant store, a candy store, a bakery, a tattoo parlor, a grocery store, a school. The sidewalks are wide and dotted with old-fashioned streetlights. The buildings are made of brick. There are trees everywhere, lining the walkways and leaning in from the woods. There's an overgrown quality to this place that makes it feel like it was abandoned for a long time.

When the bigfoot finishes his tour, he sits you down on the same bench as before. Then he tells you the most shocking thing you've heard all day: He says that you can move here if you'd like. That you can give up your old life and make a new one in this town.

He says Cryptid Creek chose you, chose to let you in. That the town itself—not the citizens, but something deeper, some consciousness under the loam and bedrock—decides who gets to find this place. And the Creek is good at picking people who need a fresh start. People who feel somehow separate from those around them, who have been looking for a place where they fit.

If you move here, you'll be part of something larger than yourself, he explains. Everyone in the Creek looks after each other. It's no utopia—there are long lines at the coffee shop and rainy days and a higher-than-average chance of running into an ex—but it's something. If you decide you want to stay here, the Creek would be happy to have you.

You don't know what to say. Can you find this place again if you need to go home and pack?

The bigfoot nods. Everyone can come and go as they please. Once you've found the Creek, you can always find it again. And it's easier to find the more you come back. But—and this goes without saying—you can't tell anyone about this place. You can't bring anyone in that the Creek didn't choose.

You nod slowly, taking this all in. A swamp monster bikes past. A yeti stops to chat with your handsome bigfoot while you think. Clouds drift lazily through the sky. It's already hard to remember what it was like in the woods. It's already hard to remember what it was like anywhere but here. But you're kind of okay with that. Here feels like a really good place. Here might even be the place for you. Why are you thinking so much? Answer the handsome bigfoot. Tell him you want to live here. And then, maybe, if you're still feeling brave, you can ask him out to dinner.

THE MOON AND THE MOTHMAN

Lucy ordered a peppermint tea and found a table near the window of their favorite coffee shop. It was a nice day outside, breezy in that early fall way that always felt like a relief. Everyone was out enjoying the weather, visiting the thrift store across the street and wandering in and out of the plant shop. Lucy watched as a bigfoot walked past the window and paused outside the bookstore.

Javalope was the best (and, okay, only) coffee shop in town, and Lucy was excited to have an excuse to come in a lot. They had just opened a bookstore next door with their best friend, Cleo. Even though Cryptid Creek was a small town, their bookstore, Bookwraith, was rarely empty. Lucy was glad for the afternoon lull. It gave them a chance to sit and chill for a minute.

Lucy blew the steam from their peppermint tea and took a sip. The sunlight coming in the window was warm on their face. The shop was filled with the sharp scent of espresso. Their chair

Mothman

creaked as they leaned away from the window.

The patrons of the coffee shop were a mix of human and cryptid. A few chupacabras sat together in the corner, and toward the middle of the room a nightcrawler was having lunch with a girl in a cute floral dress. Those two were in here a lot, and Lucy had been trying to determine if they were a couple or just friends.

The scream of the espresso machine drew Lucy's attention to the counter, where the real reason for their visit was pulling a shot.

There he was: Mothman, a cloud of steam from the espresso machine rising around him, the little silver hoops in his antennae flashing in the sunlight. He was over seven feet tall, with his fuzzy antennae easily adding another foot.

Today, he wore a distressed black sweater with the sleeves rolled up to his forearms, and a little black beanie with holes cut for his antennae. This was Lucy's favorite of his outfits. The way his rolled-up sleeves exposed just enough of his arms and the black fuzz that covered them. The way his pants were cropped cutely at the ankle. The way his powdery wings were folded shyly against his back.

Lucy sighed. Coming to Javalope to gaze longingly at Mothman was quickly becoming their favorite hobby. There was something inherently frightening about Mothman, but that only made him hotter to Lucy. His height, his silence, the way his face was strangely indiscernible behind his huge, glowing red eyes. The mixture of attraction and fear made their heart race.

Mothman finished making the coffee and came around the counter, gingerly holding a mug. His antennae flicked in all directions as he moved. Their eyes met for a second before Lucy glanced away, chills running down their spine. Lucy could always tell when he was looking at them. The feeling raised the hair on the back of their neck like when they were outside after dark and a branch snapped just out of sight.

They put their mug down and tried to focus on anything in the room but Mothman. They could feel him getting closer, could hear the soft padding of his sneakers over all the other sounds in the room. They clipped up their bob to get their hair out of their eyes.

Lucy jumped when a mug crashed to the ground next to them. They sat up to see what had happened and found themself face-to-face with Mothman. They stuttered, their heart pounding in their ears. From this close, Lucy noticed that his compound eyes sparkled subtly as their facets caught the light.

Mothman broke their gaze and bent down to pick the broken cup up off the ground. It took Lucy a beat to realize that the broken mug he was holding was theirs.

"Oh my god, did I break that?" they asked, embarrassment snapping them out of their dreamy haze. Their cheeks burned. But Mothman just shook his head. He rubbed his wing sheepishly and Lucy realized he must have nudged their drink off the table by mistake. They could not imagine caring less. He could knock every tea they ever drank off of every table they ever sat at if it meant they got to be near him.

A wave of hot, nervous energy churned through Lucy, and somehow they knew the feeling had come from Mothman. They couldn't explain how they knew this, except to say that it didn't feel like their particular brand of anxiety. Lucy knew the way their own anxiety moved through their body, and this felt different. Mothman was holding his wings tight against his back, his head tilted down toward the floor. *He* was embarrassed now. Lucy stifled a laugh and Mothman looked up. The anxious feeling was stronger when he was looking at them.

"Don't be sorry. This is the best thing that's happened to me all day." The words were out before Lucy could stop them. They bit their lip as Mothman's antennae quirked questioningly. Then, a strange rasping sound came from somewhere in the dark abyss of Mothman's face. The sound bubbled out of him quickly and Lucy felt the same wave of heat as before. He was . . . giggling? Giggling nervously, even? He ran his free hand over his antennae as if to collect himself. He pointed at the broken mug in his hand and then at the counter.

"Peppermint tea, thanks," Lucy said. Mothman gave a thumbs-up and Lucy responded with a double thumbs-up, which would have been embarrassing except they felt another wave of warmth, this time less like a sharp ray of heat and more like the fizz of soda bubbles in their chest. Mothman's antennae quivered like he was holding back another laugh. They liked that they could make him laugh.

Mothman turned back to the counter. Lucy watched him leave, feeling themself slipping back into a dreamy haze. He walked with a loping gait that made him look like he was on the moon. His wings were slightly uneven, the right wing sitting higher on his shoulder than the left, which just barely touched the ground as he walked. They could still feel heat flickering in their chest.

"Yeah, he's into you," said Cleo. Lucy was glad they were turned away from Cleo so she couldn't see them blush. The two were in the bookstore, shelving books and rearranging displays before they opened for the day.

"Are you sure, though? Maybe he acts that way around everybody," Lucy said, turning from the books they were shelving to look at Cleo.

"Not believing that someone who obviously has a crush on you actually has a crush on you is such a Lucy move," Cleo said, rolling her eyes. "This is just like in the third grade when Ally Peters only gave you a Valentine's Day card and didn't give one to anyone else—"

"It was Valentine's Day!"

"Or in high school when that hot band kid kept asking you to practice together—"

"He was really bad at reading music."

"Or in college when you kept calling me to ask what it meant when your onstage girlfriend wanted to 'work on your stage kiss' outside of rehearsal—"

"I wanted to do a good job in the play!"

Cleo sighed. "I mean, I'm not a mind reader. But it sounds like he might have a crush." She winked and Lucy grinned, adjusting their baseball cap.

"How do I find out for sure?" Lucy asked. This was why it was so nice having Cleo for a friend. She was fluent in the language of romance and she always knew just the right thing to say in order to make someone fall in love with her.

"You have to make a move," Cleo said. Lucy frowned and bit their lip. "You don't have to do anything big. Just ask him to come by the bookstore sometime. You have to get to know him better if you ever want anything to happen."

Lucy sighed. They still weren't convinced that Mothman had been hitting on them. But maybe it was worth it to try something, just this one time. And an invitation to the bookstore wasn't exactly high stakes. They owned the bookstore! If he wasn't interested, he would assume they were just trying to get new customers.

"I could do that," they said finally.

"You could and you can and you will," said Cleo. "In fact, I think now might be a good time to grab a coffee before we open." Cleo shelved one last book and spun toward the door. "Come on, I'll go with you. I'll be your wingman." Lucy finished their display and met Cleo at the door.

"You have to be really chill," they said, "you have to be a chill wingman. And you're not allowed to kick me."

Cleo feigned shock. "First of all, I know you. I know how you operate. I would only ever be a chill wingman to you. Second of all, I have never kicked you in my life." Lucy rolled their eyes and pushed Cleo ("Pushing! You're the aggressive one!") out the door.

In the coffee shop, Lucy's mood lifted as soon as they caught a glimpse of Mothman's antennae over the espresso machine. Lucy and Cleo stepped up to the register. Mothman wiped off the milk steamer on the espresso machine and turned around to face them. As soon as he saw Lucy, his antennae fluttered and he held his wings a little straighter. Cleo kicked the back of Lucy's leg.

"Hi, um," Lucy started, getting distracted when they noticed the red light coming from his eyes getting brighter. Cleo kicked them again. "I'll have a drip coffee, please," they finally managed.

"I'll have a matcha latte," Cleo said, digging her wallet out of her pocket. Mothman's eyes flicked to her briefly, then back to Lucy. He nodded and grabbed cups. "Lucy and I wanted to grab a coffee before the store opens. Have you been to our bookstore?" Cleo asked. Mothman shook his head, his eyes flicking back to Lucy before he turned to make their drinks. "That's okay, we haven't been open too long," Cleo said. Lucy watched Mothman's wings move against the back of his black T-shirt as he worked.

"You should come by sometime," Lucy said, "I could recommend you something good." Mothman's antennae lifted and he glanced over his shoulder. A sensation like a cool breeze swept through Lucy. The feeling was gentle and refreshing; a small relief. In his own way, Mothman was smiling. The room suddenly felt much quieter. Lucy smiled back.

"Anyway, we're right next door. Stop in if you have time,"

they said, trying to sound nonchalant. Then: "I hope you can come by." Another wave of cool that almost managed to stop Lucy's blush.

Mothman nodded as he put the two to-go cups on the counter. His eyes looked even brighter than usual. Cleo paid and grabbed both cups and headed for the door. Lucy was following when they felt a thrill run down their spine. They turned and saw that Mothman was still looking at them. He didn't turn away when they noticed him. Instead, he raised one long-fingered hand and waved. A tangle of emotions roiled through their chest, delight and embarrassment and longing and pleasure, so that Lucy felt giddy as they waved back. A thought struck them as they turned to go: Were those Lucy's feelings, or were they Mothman's? Their heart swelled at the possibility.

A few days passed before Mothman visited. But one day, finally, the bell over the door tinkled and there he was. Lucy took a deep breath as he lowered his antennae to fit through the doorway. When he caught them watching him, Lucy felt him smile. They smiled back.

"Lucy, do you have—" Cleo started as she walked out of the back room. She stopped when she saw Mothman. "Actually, never mind. Hi, Mothman," Cleo said quickly as she hurried back into the back room.

Mothman smiled again, his eyes scanning around the store. It felt surreal to have him here, in their bookstore, the place they'd worked so hard to put together. Every book on the shelves had been carefully chosen by Lucy and Cleo, every shelf put up by them. The couch in the back corner had come from their first apartment. Bookwraith was an extension of the two of them, of their friendship. Mothman trailed a long finger across several books in a display and Lucy shivered.

"You like fantasy novels, too?" they asked, walking to stand next to him. He tapped the cover of a book. *Howl's Moving Castle,* one of Lucy's all-time favorites. A trill of delight ran through them. Mothman stood up straighter as if in response to their feeling, the ends of his antennae twining together. Lucy tucked a lock of dark hair behind their ear.

"Have you read this one?" Lucy asked, picking up another book from the table. Mothman shook his head. "Oh, you have to read *Tehanu.* But maybe you should start at the beginning of the series? It's right over here," Lucy wandered to the fantasy section. They found the book and turned to hand it to Mothman, only to find him standing right behind them. Lucy's mouth went dry as they held out the book.

He was so close to Lucy that they could smell not only his vetiver cologne, but the musky, earthy smell underneath. They felt goosebumps erupt down their arms and their breathing became suddenly shallow. Between his height and his wings and his bright, bright eyes, he seemed to surround them. Like the world was all just Mothman, just dark fur and dusty wings and black high-tops. Was it possible to loom in a cute way?

Mothman took the book from them, and turned it over to

read the back cover. Neither of them moved. Lucy took a slow, deep breath in and their chest nearly touched Mothman's elbow. They tried to clear their head and realized they could feel that same hot roil of emotions that they'd felt in the coffee shop, the fear and the yearning, and this time—something hungrier. A hunger that made their mouth go dry and their stomach bottom out. These feelings were coming from Mothman. He was an emotional radio tower and Lucy was tuned to his frequency. They took another deep breath.

His antennae moved absently as he read. Lucy had the sudden urge to run their hand through the fuzz covering his antennae. They felt their hand twitch, and had to grab the bookshelf to stop themself from reaching for him. Mothman looked down at the sudden movement and locked eyes with Lucy.

They stood like that for a moment: maybe a few breaths, maybe half a year, Lucy couldn't tell anymore. Mothman's eyes got brighter the longer he looked at them. Lucy wasn't in the bookstore anymore, they were floating somewhere in the dark pit of night where the only light came from Mothman's eyes.

He was extremely tall, so they had to tilt their chin nearly to the ceiling to keep eye contact. He seemed to be standing even closer than before. Lucy could hear him breathing, could feel the hair on their arms standing on end as though he was exerting a static presence. They imagined a crackle of electric light jumping between them. The bell over the door tinkled. Lucy gasped. Mothman blinked and took a step back.

"I can help you!" Cleo yelped, racing from the back of the

store to deal with the customer. Lucy had the distinct sense she had been spying from the inventory room, but at the moment they didn't care. Mothman's antennae stood straight up, alert, and they held up the book.

"You want to buy it?" Lucy asked, and Mothman nodded. "Sure thing, I can ring you up," they said. They were grateful for the normalcy of business to snap them out of their stupor. They were selling a book, they worked in a bookstore, their name was Lucy and their hands were a normal amount sweaty. These were facts.

They led Mothman to the counter and rang him up. Their heart was pounding the whole time, and they could feel that Mothman's heart was pounding too. He was emitting a hiccupy warmth that felt at once comfortable and restless. When he left the store and the door closed behind him, Lucy spent a long time staring after him. That was something. That was definitely something.

After his first visit, Mothman started coming into the store on a regular basis. Sometimes he would shop, sometimes he would just hang out with Lucy and Cleo. His favorite thing seemed to be getting book recommendations from Lucy.

It would go like this: Mothman would come in, and no matter where in the store Lucy was, they would immediately know he was there. At first, Lucy would rush out right away to see him. Once it became clear that stopping by was a habit for Mothman, they would take a minute finishing whatever task they were working on and let him browse or chat with Cleo (who was getting decent at interpreting his vibes-based communication style).

As soon as Lucy was within Mothman's line of sight, Lucy would feel butterflies flutter all through their body and the temperature in the room would go up a few degrees. They would collect themself as best they could and walk up to him and try to say something and not just stand there staring at him with a lovestruck look on their face.

The more time Lucy spent with Mothman, the better they got at understanding him. It wasn't quite like learning a new language; it was more like watching a morning fog slowly clear. Their communication was originally limited to Mothman sending general feelings to Lucy, but now Lucy could see images and wisps of memory in their head when they talked to Mothman. After a few weeks, they could have full conversations like this.

When he wanted a recommendation, Mothman would show Lucy a feeling or a series of images and Lucy would scramble around the bookstore with him as they tried to find a book that matched the vibe he'd asked for. Sometimes it was a vague feeling, like being inside on a stormy day. Sometimes it was something more specific, a clip from a movie he liked or a particular type of story he was looking for. In this way, Lucy learned about his favorite books and movies and hobbies, and told him about their own as well. They knew he preferred horror but also loved romance, and he knew Lucy was particularly good at recommending historical fiction and fantasy (and magical girl manga).

While Lucy scanned the shelves, he'd stand nearby, always close enough that they could smell his vetiver scent and feel his gaze on their back. This was Lucy's favorite part of the process.

When they found him a book, Mothman would smile and let his fingers linger on Lucy's as they handed it to him. He'd buy a copy and the next time Lucy was in the coffee shop they'd see him paging through it during slow shifts. They had the sense he wanted them to see him reading it.

These moments were almost painfully romantic. Watching Mothman lean against the counter, his apron tied messily around his waist, his sleeves rolled to his elbows and his long fingers skimming the soft pages. There was nothing in the world more distracting than watching Mothman read. Lucy was getting used to room-temperature coffee.

"It's erotic," Cleo said.

Lucy and Cleo were having a movie night. Or, they were supposed to be having a movie night. They had only made it five minutes into the B horror movie that Lucy had pirated before they paused it to talk about Mothman. The TV screen was frozen on a still of a beautiful woman covered in radioactive goo.

"It's not *erotic*," Lucy groaned. "It's cute. He's reading the books I picked out for him."

"No, it's erotic. I see the way you look at each other. I *feel* the way he looks at you. It's like he's a moon in your orbit, but in a sexy way. Like if the moon orbited the earth because it wanted to make out with it."

Lucy laughed. "I'd want to make out with the moon if I were the earth," they said.

"Well, you *are* the earth and Mothman *is* the moon and you *do* want to french each other until you combust or turn into black holes or whatever it is that planets do," Cleo said, flicking Lucy's shoulder. Lucy blushed.

"It's not *not* erotic," they said finally. Cleo rolled her eyes.

"Thank you for admitting it."

"He's just so . . . tall," Lucy said dreamily.

"And his T-shirts are always just the right amount of worn out," Cleo sighed.

"And his wings are all silvery in the light,"

"And his eyes—"

"His eyes!" Lucy yelled, covering their face with their hand. "Cleo, did you know that when you stand really close to Mothman, the light from his eyes is warm?" they said from under their hand.

"Whoa," Cleo said.

"Yeah," Lucy said. They both sighed and sunk lower into the couch. "Erotic," Lucy whispered.

As soon as Lucy walked into Javalope, Mothman was looking at them, his antennae standing straight up. Lucy bit their lip and waved. It was becoming increasingly difficult to pretend they just wanted to be friends with Mothman. It was becoming abundantly clear that Mothman didn't want to be just friends either. Lucy could feel it in the gust of heat that came off him every time they stood close.

Yesterday Mothman had showed them a memory of Lucy's own freckled hands scratching the frog tattoo on their bicep. It was such a small moment, so forgettable, but Lucy could feel the worn edges around the end of the memory, as though Mothman had been holding it in his back pocket and looking at it often. Thinking about it sent them into a hot, full-body blush. It was time for Lucy to make a real move—an idea that both scared and excited them.

They walked up to the counter, Mothman's eyes following them the whole time.

"You get off soon, right?" they asked. Mothman nodded. "Let's go somewhere when you're done." Mothman showed them a picture of the bookstore and Cleo, his antennae tilted questioningly. Lucy took a breath. "No, let's go somewhere just you and me," they said. Their eyes flicked nervously away from his. They felt a familiar nervous warmth shiver through them. When they finally managed to look back up at him, his eyes were bright. He nodded and they felt him smile. Lucy smiled back. Their shoulders relaxed. "Cool. I'll be over there whenever you're ready to go," they said, pointing to a table in the corner. Mothman sent a little jolt of excitement. Lucy smiled again and ordered a drip coffee. They settled down at a worn-out wooden table to read.

A movement on the other side of the table startled them a few minutes later. Mothman was standing there, looking at them.

"Ready to go?" they asked as they stood up and stretched. Mothman's gaze flickered to the strip of exposed skin on their stomach that showed when their shirt rode up. His antennae twitched. It calmed Lucy down a bit. This was the right move. They led him to the door.

"I was thinking we could grab Thai food or something," Lucy said, stepping outside and hooking a thumb up the street toward the Thai place. Mothman nodded, then tilted his head with a question. He wanted to bring Lucy somewhere first. He wouldn't show them where they were going, he just nodded down the street in the opposite direction. Lucy figured they were already in this deep, they might as well go with it. They nodded and followed Mothman into the oncoming dark.

The day had turned into a warm evening. The sky was dusky, the last edges of sunset still visible on the horizon. The air was sweet with cottonwood and pine. Mothman slowed down so Lucy could keep up with him, and for a while they just walked together in silence.

Lucy had always liked this time of night, the time when it was still just bright enough to see but dark enough that the sky was a dusty, luminous blue. The time of night when the streetlights turned on.

As they walked, they snuck glances at Mothman. In the dark, his eyes glowed even brighter. He had a slow, slightly uneven gait that made him seem relaxed, but Lucy could tell by the way he held his wings that he was nervous. They could feel him sneaking glances at them, could see the beam from his spotlight eyes. Whenever Lucy felt his gaze flicker to them, they melted a little bit.

They walked for a while, eventually leaving town and following a trail through the dense woods. The sky grew darker between the treetops, but the light from Mothman's eyes led the way.

Finally, they stepped into a clearing and Mothman's antennae stood straight up. Before them was an old wooden bridge with a quiet stream passing underneath it. The only sounds were the burbling and swirling noises of the stream and the singing of bugs in the trees. Tufts of wildflowers and ferns grew on either side of the bridge.

Mothman gently touched Lucy's shoulder. They felt all the blood in their body rush to the point of contact. Before they could even process the touch, Mothman was walking away, moving to the middle of the bridge. He sat down on the side of the bridge, his legs hanging over the water. For a moment, Lucy just watched him. The long lines of his body, the subtle shimmer of his wings. The moon peeked over the trees and outlined him in silver.

Lucy ran a hand through their hair to shake themself out of their stupor, and then walked to the bridge and sat down next to him. Their freckled legs hung over the water, close enough to brush against Mothman's legs if Lucy wanted to.

"Do you come here a lot?" Lucy asked, watching the river ripple in the moonlight. Mothman nodded, also looking out at the water. He pointed to a spot by Lucy's leg. In the soft wood, there was a small carving in the shape of a moth. Lucy ran a finger over the carving and Mothman's antennae shivered. They traced the outline again just to watch him shiver.

Lucy could feel, for the first time, a deep sense of calm radiating from Mothman. There was none of the skittery heat or the unruly tangle of feelings that usually accompanied him. There was only a soft coolness, almost indistinguishable from the night air. They realized that although Mothman had been to their special place—the bookstore—countless times now, they had never been to a place that was special to him. The coffee shop was, of course, the place that Lucy most associated with him. But that was just where he worked, it wasn't the place he came when he wanted a quiet moment or needed to think.

They were struck at once by how vulnerable Mothman was. He didn't talk, but his feelings were always being telegraphed to the people around him. He had some control over it, and not everyone knew him well enough to see his thoughts the way Lucy could, but it was still such a delicate way to live. So close to the skin.

They shifted slightly so their leg was touching Mothman's. The feeling of his jeans against their bare skin made Lucy bite their lip. They watched their boots dangling over the water, saw when Mothman bumped his leg meaningfully against theirs.

When they looked up, Mothman was watching them. They suddenly had a vision of their own face, in this moment, bathed in red light and staring up at Mothman. Their face looked familiar but also strange, filtered not just through Mothman's eyes, but also his thoughts. An overwhelming rush of warmth ran through them as they saw their uneven lips, their DIY haircut, the patch of acne on their chin, all rendered in a soft glow.

The image made Lucy feel disoriented and flushed and dizzy with a longing so powerful it hurt. They blinked and the vision was gone; they were once again looking up at Mothman's big eyes.

Lucy was breathless. They'd never experienced anything so intimate and tender. It was strange to see themself from the outside, but also enthralling. It was a direct hit of Mothman's feelings for them. Lucy wanted more. They wanted to return the favor, to show Mothman exactly how they felt about him. They didn't want to wait anymore. They reached up and pulled Mothman's face to theirs.

Kissing Mothman was like stepping into a heavy fog. The feeling wasn't lips on lips. Rather, Lucy felt like they had dipped their face in a fast-moving river; a cool sensation started in their mouth and flowed quickly through the rest of their body.

Every now and then a flash of sensation would twist through their body and they would feel the kiss from Mothman's point of view. They felt Mothman slide his fingers into their hair, but they also felt the warmth of their own scalp in Mothman's hands. They felt his jaw moving against their palms, but they also felt the spark of want in Mothman when they slid a thumb over his furry cheek.

Lucy vanished into the kiss. They were in their body and Mothman's body all at once, and they melted into the waves of sensation that swept over them. Mothman's hand was on their waist and their hand was running down his chest and they were passing the same spark of want back and forth between them so that a glowing heat consumed them both.

When Lucy finally opened their eyes, they realized they were now lying on the bridge. They didn't remember changing position. Mothman lay next to them, radiating heat and looking dazed. They were both breathing heavily.

Fireflies were out now. The water echoed as it ran under the bridge. Lucy reached out and ran a hand over one of Mothman's antennae. Moonlight scattered off his eyes. Lucy could feel the throb of Mothman's thoughts. They knew he could feel theirs too. The exchange of feelings was more automatic than conversation, more instinctive, like moving to scratch an itch. Something so innate it could be done in sleep.

Mothman took a shaky breath when Lucy thought about the kiss and the wanting that came before. They had a vision of their own fingers with their own chewed-up nails accompanied by a rush of heat. Lucy felt like they were in a dream.

Eventually, they rolled onto their back to look at the stars. They took Mothman's hand and their heart fluttered at the feeling of his fuzzy palms. Lucy smiled, and they could feel him smiling too. Overhead, the moon was bright.

A NEW LEAF

I looked at the window over my kitchen sink. It was a perfect spring afternoon. The sun was bright and golden and the sky was white-blue. Nearly every day of the last thirty years, I've looked out my kitchen window to see the Loveland Frog in her own kitchen, living out the various phases of domestic life. I've seen her wandering pregnant around her kitchen, strapping her son into his high chair, reading to her daughter. Then she was getting them ready for school while her husband made their lunches. I've seen her celebrate birthdays and graduations and I've seen her being held by her husband after she came home from my husband's wake. I've seen her fashion change from tailored button-ups to swaths of loose florals.

I've seen her standing over her sink, drinking coffee out of a small bowl (in the European style, she always tells me). I've seen her fix her lipstick and spill oatmeal on her sweater and wave good morning to me. And I know she's seen all these things from me as well. Our lives have been so entangled for the last three decades that in some ways I feel like I was married to her as much as I was married to my late husband. We spent weekends and evenings together, organized playdates for our kids, taught each other recipes and gossiped and drank and gave gifts. We did all the things that make up a life, and we did so many of them together.

Today was the day, after weeks of planning, that Lovey was moving in with me. For the first time, my window looked into an empty house. Even though I was excited to get to live with my best friend, I was also nervous. I've always hoped to be the kind of person that Loveland naturally is—someone who doesn't need help, who knows how to do everything perfectly. With my husband and daughter, I could pretend at being that person. With Loveland it was different. It was harder to hide.

There was a knock at my front door and I took a deep breath before I went to answer it. In the doorway was Loveland. She looked casually elegant as always in a floral linen dress and a big green scarf, her silver hair held back by a large clip. Her liquid frog's eyes were bright and her large mouth was pulled into a smile. In the spring sunlight, her soft green skin seemed to glow.

"It's today!" she said, her throaty voice croaking with enthusiasm.

"Finally!" I replied, hoping I was smiling as big as she was. I stepped to the side and invited her in. We'd spent the last month moving all her things from her house over to mine, but now Lovey herself was here to stay. I wrapped my arms around her as soon as she crossed the threshold. She was soft and warm and slightly damp. She smelled as she always did: like patchouli and a bit of dirt. She hugged me as tightly as I hugged her. When we finally let go of each other, we giggled like children.

“Let me show you to your chambers,” I said with a slight bow. We both laughed and she followed me down the hall to the room across from mine. It used to be my daughter’s room, but Bridget hasn’t lived at home in years. When Lovey and I told her our plan, she was happy to give up her room. It had taken me and Bridget a while to get all her Cranberries band posters off the wall and her boxes of old sketchbooks out of the closet, but her room was finally ready for Lovey to move in. We’d painted the walls a light greenish gray. On the desk under the window, I’d put a photo of Lovey and me at her son’s high school graduation. It was a small room, but it was nice. I made sure it was nice.

“My god. It looks perfect, Lillian,” she said when she entered the room. “It’s been so long since I had my own bedroom. And this one has no bad memories attached.”

Lovey’s divorce was the catalyst for this move. I had never particularly liked Ed. I didn’t understand what Lovey saw in him. He was so ordinary and she’s always been exceptional.

“What smells so good? Are you roasting a chicken?” she asked when we sat down in the living room. I preened under her praise. I knew she liked my cooking.

“Roast chicken is the perfect special occasion food,” I said. She smiled.

“I’m glad I’m still a special occasion,” she said.

We sat in comfortable silence for a few minutes while the sun started peeking in the windows and the smell of rosemary floated through the house. I was so happy to be here with her. The worries I'd had over the last few weeks vanished as we sat together. Lovey wasn't some model of perfection—she was my friend. I promised myself I'd be less envious, that I wouldn't let my own fears of inadequacy get in the way of this relationship.

I looked across the room at her. A strand of her gray hair had fallen out of her clip and hung by her cheek. I imagined getting up and tucking it behind her ear, my fingers brushing her gooey frog skin. I felt myself blush. Loveland reached into a bag at her side and withdrew her pipe. When she lit a match, the small flame reflected in her eyes.

My ruined garden had been a sore spot for me for years. When my husband was alive, he spent all his free time turning our small backyard into a work of art. Herb built a row of standing beds that lined the fence, scattered wildflower seeds in the grass, hung baskets of flowers over the back patio. I still remembered what he would grow in each bed: Marigolds and dahlias in one square, squash and beans in another. One of the beds was all herbs, one was pansies and snapdragons. He filled the space with bright flowers and big vegetables and every shade of green. Now it was nothing but a graying patch of weeds. I felt guilty every time I looked out the back door.

So when Lovey brought up the idea of fixing up the garden, it felt like she'd dug a pair of pruning shears into my chest.

"It wouldn't be *that* much work," she said. We were sitting in the kitchen about a week after she moved in. I'd fixed us breakfast and we'd been having a perfectly nice time until she brought up all the dead plants she could see just outside the French doors. "It's not like we're doing anything else," she added when I didn't answer.

"I don't think we need to do anything—it's not like it's so bad," I said. I avoided looking at her.

"It's not great, Lillian," she said. I bit my cheek. Loveland had no way to know that the garden had become such an emotional bruise for me. I reminded myself that she wasn't trying to be mean, that she lived here now and had as much right to the space as I did.

"I don't know much about gardening. It would have to be your project," I said.

"That's okay. You can just sit inside and watch me plant flowers and bring me lemonade every now and then." She smiled big. I grimaced back.

"It would be a lot of damn work," I said. She rolled her eyes.

"This is my garden now too, and I want to make it nice," she said. I watched Lovey watching me and we both knew I was about to give in.

"Just go work on your garden," I said. An excited gleam flashed across Lovey's face and she leapt up from the table, suddenly spry.

"My garden!" she cried, and she hurried down the hall to

change. I sat at the table, trying not to look outside. I felt exhausted. I felt afraid that I would never do anything right. I got up to put our plates in the sink. I looked out the window into her now-dark house. In the dim glass, I saw my own reflection.

It took a good few days for Loveland to clear the weeds out. It hadn't been as painful as I'd expected. It was nice seeing someone out working in the garden. It had been so long since I'd been able to glance out the window and see someone out there. Loveland worked without order or method, keeping her gardening tools in a messy pile in the middle of the yard and pulling up weeds at random. Every now and then, she'd absentmindedly flick out her tongue and catch a fly. I always smiled to myself when I caught her doing this. I'd bring her lemonade and she'd complain about her knees and then she'd go right back to pulling weeds until it was dark out. I came to enjoy our little routine.

The trouble came when we finished the job and I had to look at the newly clean garden. Seeing it without the weeds, I remembered how beautiful it had once been and I felt guilty for letting it all go. Tears pricked the corners of my eyes, but I held them back.

"Mom," Bridget called from the back door. I came back to myself and turned to see my daughter and Loveland watching me. "I brought those bags of soil, I'm gonna get them out of the truck." I nodded and she turned back into the house.

"It's already looking a lot better out here," I said. Lovey

smiled a shit-eating grin.

"Do you think a tidy yard looks better than one that's absolutely overrun with weeds and dead plants?" she asked teasingly.

"For Christ's sake, Lovey," I muttered. The words must have come out sharper than I'd expected, because she flashed me a concerned look.

"Is everything okay?" she asked. I gave her a forced smile. She wasn't trying to be rude. It was just a garden.

"I think I'm just hungry. I'll go make some lunch," I said. Lovey's gaze searched my face and she nodded uncertainly. I willed my smile to be real. Lovey looked like she was going to say something else, but just then Bridget came out of the house with another bag of soil. I left Lovey to tell her where to put it and went inside.

I made myself a sandwich and sat at the kitchen table, watching Lovey and Bridget fill the garden beds with fresh soil. I felt that I was watching two alternate versions of myself—one version of me who was young and kind and eager to give, another version who was my age, but wiser and more thoughtful, lovelier and more sympathetic. And then there was the real me, watching and unable to join.

A week later, Lovey was in the backyard filling up the first garden bed. We'd decided on a mix of poppies for this one. Their papery petals looked so pretty in the sunlight. Lovey wore a wide-brimmed straw hat. I sat on the patio and watched her work. As with her weeding, her planting wasn't particularly organized. It seemed like she was trying to make rows, but they weren't coming out quite right. We'd been sitting in silence for a while when Lovey spoke.

"Jack called this morning," she said.

"What's he up to these days?" I asked.

"He just got back from visiting his dad," she said. I leaned a little forward in my chair.

"Oh?" I said. Loveland kept digging.

"He said it was nice. Jack said Ed likes the city." I kept looking at Lovey and she kept not looking at me. Her gaze was fixed on the garden bed. "You try your damndest to plant these things evenly, and they still come out looking a mess," she muttered. Then, without warning, she dug her fingers into the soil and ripped out a poppy by the roots.

The movement was so sudden and violent that my breath caught in my throat. She'd spent most of breakfast talking about how excited she was to plant these poppies, how lovely and delicate they were. I watched as she clenched the poppy's roots in her hand, bits of soil falling to the ground. Lovey had never been one to hide her feelings. Even so, I'd rarely seen her so visibly upset.

"To be clear, I'm happy for Ed," she said. She pulled out another poppy. I watched quietly, nervously. "And I'm happy the kids still have a good relationship with him," she continued. Another poppy. The roots made a muffled tearing sound as she pulled. Her fingers were caked with black dirt. "I'm happy about those things, and also"—here she finally turned to me—"I'm not happy."

I didn't say anything, just looked at her. She was crouched like she was ready to jump. Her eyes were tired and her gaze was unfocused, even as she looked at me. I had often wondered how it must feel to have an emotion and be able to express it immediately without fear of judgment or repercussion. I realized for the first time the incredible vulnerability that this required.

I had always feared that expressing painful emotions would make other people uncomfortable or overburdened. But as I got up and hurried over to Loveland, as I kneeled next to her in the dirt without a second thought, I realized that I had never felt that way when Lovey shared her emotions with me. I'd only ever felt glad to hear how she felt. Even if she was upset, I felt grateful that she would share with me. Taking care of Loveland never felt like a burden to me.

"What do you need right now?" I asked. I was nervous to ask this, annoyed at myself for not knowing, deeply and instinctively, how to help her. But more than that, I was worried about Lovey and I wanted badly to make her feel better. Her eyes focused like she was coming back from a long distance away.

"I need these flowers to be in actual rows," she said. I nodded.

"Why don't you pull them all out and I'll fix them later," I said. She glanced at me uncertainly. "It's your garden. If you want to yank up all the poppies you can yank up all the poppies. I don't mind cleaning up after you," I said. I felt my face grow warm. Lovey looked from me to the flowers and back again, and then started pulling up poppies in an unrestrained frenzy.

A cloud of dirt hung in the air around her, and papery orange poppy petals settled in her hair. I sat back and watched.

When she finally finished, she was absolutely covered in soil and bits of flower. Everything stuck to her slightly wet skin. She breathed heavily and her long, pink tongue snapped above her head suddenly to catch a passing fly. Her eyes were wild, but they looked a little less tired.

"How was that?" I asked.

"I think poppies might be my favorite flower," she said. I laughed and she cracked a grin.

Lovey went inside and slept for a long, long time. The longest since she moved in. While she was asleep, I replanted the garden. I found myself enjoying the work much more than I'd expected. Planting wasn't easy work, but it was quiet and repetitive and I liked the feeling of my spade in the soil. Even when my knees and back started to hurt, I kept at it.

I liked how simple it was to dig a hole, to place a flower in it. I liked the feeling of the sun on my back, even though I was hot and sweaty. I like the feeling of the cool evening air, even when the bugs came out. I liked feeling like this was something Lovey and I were doing together, even though she wasn't here. I spent extra time making sure my rows were even.

After that, I started helping Lovey in the garden. We raked and seeded and fertilized and watered and about a month after we'd started our project, I looked out the open French doors and saw our garden beds full of budding flowers and fresh soil. There were bleeding hearts and peonies and poppies and wild roses. Forget-me-nots and irises and tall, yellow globe flowers. One bed was full of chives and mint and rosemary. Hanging baskets by the door overflowed with fuchsias and geraniums. There were snapdragons in a pot near the bench at the back of the yard. Lovey and I had watered everything that morning, and the petals and leaves glittered in the sun.

Looking at the finished product, I suddenly found that my eyes were wet with tears. I hadn't been expecting to cry. A tangle of emotions twisted in my chest: grief and joy and shame. I couldn't believe it had taken me this long to fix the garden. I was embarrassed that I hadn't fixed it on my own. More than anything else, though, I was grateful to Lovey for pushing me—pushing us both—to create something so beautiful. I was so glad to have her here, with me.

"What do you think?" Lovey asked from behind me. I turned to look at her, eyes full of tears. As soon as she saw my face she wrapped me up in a hug. We didn't speak at first, just stood in the kitchen holding each other, my tears soaking her shoulder. Finally, I pulled back from her and wiped my face. I didn't like to cry in front of people. But in this moment, I needed her.

She held my hand and I focused on the feeling of her skin on mine; the soft-sticky texture of her skin, the way her hands slowly warmed up to my temperature, the slight damp that always exuded from her. She watched me with her liquid eyes, her concern visible on her face.

"We don't have to talk about it," she said, "but we can if you want." I took a deep breath.

So many feelings hit me at once, I couldn't think of where to begin. Another moment of silence passed.

"Thank you for fixing the garden," I said finally. I couldn't explain what it meant to me to have her here. I couldn't express the depth of my gratitude, or of my grief. I could only thank her for giving me this small gift.

"I'm really grateful that you let me help. I've loved getting to do this with you," she said. My heart fluttered. I rested my head on her shoulder again and she rubbed my back. Then, she nuzzled her face in my hair and planted a kiss on the crown of my head. She'd never done that before. My face grew warm.

"Thank you for being here," I said into her shoulder.

"Thank you for letting me be here," she said into my hair. I hugged her tighter. I wanted to be as close to her as possible.

The party was my idea. It wouldn't be anything big—just a few close friends and our kids. I like to throw parties. I think it makes life more interesting when you can always find a reason to celebrate—and we had a very good reason to celebrate. The garden was finally finished. Everything was young and fresh and clean, not yet the carefully overgrown garden that Herb had left, but someday it would get there.

"I told you it would be better like this," Lovey said, appearing suddenly at my side. For the first time, her jokes about the garden didn't bother me. It wasn't my garden anymore, or Herb's. It was something new. It was ours. I gave her a genuine smile.

"Where would I be without your guidance," I said, rolling my eyes but resting my head on her shoulder. She leaned her cheek on top of my head. We stood like that, looking at the beautiful thing we'd created together.

"I think we have everything ready for tonight," I said. I felt Lovey nod.

"We've got groceries and lights and Jack and Ellie are getting into town soon. They said they'd stay with Bridget," she said.

"It'll be nice having all of them in town," I said. Lovey nodded again.

"All of our kids," she said. I felt something well up in my chest, an emotion like a happy melancholy.

For the party, I roasted a chicken and baked a cake. Lovey made drinks and assembled a cheese board. She and Bridget had hung strings of fairy lights along the fence and I put out a few hurricane lanterns so the whole yard glowed in the early dusk. There was just enough room outside for all eight people we'd invited. At first, Loveland and I walked around and mingled with everyone, but as the night drew on we retreated to the bench. We sat together, watching our guests talk and laugh and dance.

"Why are all our friends younger than us?" I asked. She laughed as Griffin and Mitch turned up the volume on the speaker Jack had brought.

"Because otherwise we'd have nobody to dance for our entertainment," she said, and I smiled. She reached out and placed her hand over mine, squeezing it gently.

She turned to look at me then, and in her eyes I saw our entire history, our entire friendship. The dinners, the playdates, the long phone calls, the late-night conversations, the years spent watching each other from our kitchen windows. I looked out at the garden that she'd planted for me, at our children and friends laughing together in our backyard.

"Lovey," I said after a pause, "do you know that I'm in love with you?" I said it so easily, so simply, like it just slipped out of my mouth alongside my breath. Like I had said it many times before. I hadn't been expecting to say it. I hadn't even been fully aware that this was how I felt. But when I spoke the words, I knew they were true. I knew I'd been waiting to say them for a long, long time.

"Took you long enough to realize," she said, and before I could respond she pulled me in to her and kissed me gently. The kiss was slow and simple. Her lips were wet and her face was warm and she felt just how I imagined, only better. It felt like something we had done a thousand times before.

After we broke apart, I nestled into her side and we sat curled up into each other on the old wooden bench. The garden still looked so new, but I could see how it would look when it was old, too. In the years that would follow this one, I could see how it would become thoughtfully overgrown, the flowers blooming year after year, wildflowers sprouting from the grass, the herbs becoming hearty and near-wild. And I knew, no matter how much time passed, that Lovey would be beside me, curled up next to me in this garden, her eyes reflecting the light of the stars.

PRACTICE MAKES PERFECT

The door of Bookwraith bursts open and in walks a small person, mummified in a scarf and puffy jacket, swearing about how cold it is outside and laden down with a beaten-up cardboard box. Before I can say anything, the person reaches into the box, hands me a zine, and starts struggling with the scarf wrapped around their neck and head. The zine cover has a marker drawing of a broken heart above the words *Have Sex with Me: Poems by Mason*. The Mason in question is still wrestling his scarf when I read the title out loud.

"I wanted a catchy title. It's hard to get people to read poetry," he says, voice muffled. I look from the zine in my hand to the short guy in front of me currently choking himself with what looks like a very bulky, very homemade scarf. I'm having a hard time connecting the art to the artist.

I came to Bookwraith today because I haven't left the house in a week and I was starting to go insane. I always get more anx-

ZINE
Swampy

ious in the winter, and this February has been kicking my ass. I'd hoped to be a little more social after I came out as transmasc, but in the last few months I've barely left my apartment. I'm anxious because I'm happy to be out, and I'm anxious because coming out is exhausting. It's a tough cycle. It doesn't make things any easier that I'm the only trans swamp monster I know. I want to go outside and slut it up, but then I'm like, is a transmasc swamp monster supposed to slut it up? Am I bad transmasc swamp monster representation if I do that?

But today I forced myself to walk to the bookstore, because I always feel better at the bookstore. I like Cleo and Lucy a lot. I'm a little jealous that Lucy and Mothman are dating, though. I used to have the biggest crush on Mothman. I was drinking three cups of coffee a day just so I'd have lots of chances to see him. In a way, I'm glad he's dating Lucy because at least it's cut down a lot on my coffee consumption. I'm way less jittery now. Still pretty jittery, but definitely less.

Anyway, this was how I came to be holding Mason's poems and watching him fight with his scarf.

"What kind of poems are they?" I ask him.

"They're about love and sex and—" He gets his scarf off and I finally get a clear view of him. I almost miss the rest of his sentence because this guy is so hot. He's, like, main-character-in-a-Gregg-Araki-movie hot. He has hair that you can tell he's always sensually pushing out of his eyes. It's cut into a tasteful mullet. His eyes are dark and his eyelashes are stupidly long. His nose is a little snubbed. His body is one slim line, like a trail of smoke from a cigarette.

"They're about love and sex and being a pervert," he repeats. A thrill goes through me as I watch his lips form the word *pervert*.

"I'm Mason. I make zines. Mostly bad ones," he says. He walks up to me and shakes my webbed hand. He quickly reaches up to push his hair out of his eyes.

"I'm Swampy," I say, trying to sound chill.

"You like zines?" he asks. I'd never considered whether I particularly like zines, but when Mason looks up at me through his long eyelashes I nod emphatically.

"That copy is yours, on the house." He winks at me and my heart leaps into my throat.

"Before you get too excited, they only cost two dollars," Lucy says. Mason grins. He has a pretty smile, one that lights up his whole face. His canines are a little crooked in a way that makes him seem mischievous. Mischievous and hot.

"What're you up to today?" he asks me. He takes his box over to the counter and helps Lucy unload his zines.

"Trying to stave off a panic attack," I say before I can think. One good thing about being a swamp monster is that it's hard to tell when I'm blushing, on account of all the moss covering my face. Mason just laughs.

"Real," he says. "When I'm feeling anxious, I like to go out on a date." I watch him for a moment, taking in the way his hair falls over his cheekbones.

"I haven't been on a date in forever," I say. There's something about Mason that makes me want to tell him all my secrets. I feel like I could trust him with all of them.

"No way," he says, turning away from the box to look at me. I blush again as he gives me a once-over. "I feel like you should be going on tons of dates," he says. He smiles slyly as he turns away. My heart flips.

"I'm out of practice at this point," I admit. Mason takes the empty box off the counter as Lucy prints a roll of price stickers.

"You should have Mason, like, tutor you," says Cleo from the back of the store. "He goes on, like, ten dates a week. He's barely ever in town because he's so busy going on dates." Mason laughs at this.

"You're overstating it," he says, "it's not like I'm Lord Byron about to die from having too much sex. Although, I mean, I wish." Cleo and Lucy laugh.

"Honestly, I think you're an even bigger slut than I am," says Cleo.

"Sluts!" cheers Mason and the two of them high-five. I wonder how it would feel to be that relaxed around other people. To go on dates without batting an eye, to hook up regularly and without thinking about it. To have all of these experiences be as regular as doing the dishes.

Mason is looking at me curiously. I can feel his gaze like it's something physical.

"We could, if you wanted to," he says.

"Could what?" I ask.

"Go on some practice dates," he says. The room goes sideways.

"Oh, I mean—"

"I mean, I'm sure you're perfectly capable of going on real dates," he says, giving me another world-ending grin. "Just, like, if you want some practice. Something low stakes." He leans back and rests his elbows on the counter behind him. I can't believe how relaxed he is. I try to emulate his chill but my heart won't stop hammering in my chest.

"No, I didn't think—I mean, it's a cool idea," I stammer back.

"What's a practice date and how's it different from a real date?" asks Lucy. I look back to Mason, also curious what his answer will be.

"I'm not sure," he says. He runs a hand through his hair. "I'll come up with some rules, I guess."

"Nothing says romance like a list of rules," Cleo says.

"*I* think it's a cute idea," Lucy says. I also think it's a cute idea. Unbearably cute, almost. The only thing that would be better is if Mason had asked me on a real date. But I'll take what I can get.

"Here, hand me that zine for a sec," he says. I hand him back his little book of poems, now a little wet from the damp lichen on my hand. He flips it over and scribbles his number on the back. "Call me whenever you want to do this," he says as he passes it back to me. He has a nice-looking phone number.

"Thanks," I say, because I can't think of anything else. I want to call him right now, I want to go on a date with him in one minute, yesterday, last week. I try to play it cool and make up an excuse to leave the store. It's all I can do not to skip home.

When I work up the courage to call Mason, he is, as promised, very chill. He suggests dinner at Bone Broth, the ramen place. When I get there, he's already standing outside, his scarf once again wrapped around his head.

"Sorry I'm late," I say, although I know I'm five minutes early.

"You're not late," comes his muffled reply, "I got here early. I didn't want to keep you waiting." This touches me more than it has any right to. He's literally just on time, that shouldn't be a dreamy quality. And yet.

He holds open the door for me and we go inside and are shown to our table. When we sit down, he unwinds his scarf. I enjoy watching him peel off his layers like this, more and more of him coming into view as he unwraps himself. His black hair, messy from the scarf and hat, his dark eyes, a small neck tattoo of a lit match. I hadn't noticed the tattoo the other day, but now I can't stop looking at it. He's wearing a lilac crewneck sweatshirt, a sliver of white T-shirt poking up above the neckline. He runs his hand through his hair a few times trying to surreptitiously fix it, and I notice his long, perfect fingers. I choke slightly on my water.

"You good?" he asks. I nod, trying to get myself together. "Cool. Wouldn't want you to die before we even order," he says and smiles. I do an embarrassing cough-laugh. A waiter comes up to us and we order.

"Okay, so, tip number one: I like to start a date with compliments," he says. "I don't like playing hard to get and I don't like beating around the bush. I'd rather just tell you that I think you look hot and then we can both move forward with that knowledge. Otherwise I feel like we're wasting time," he explains. I nod.

"So you're saying you think I'm hot?" I ask. This isn't the kind of line I'd usually deliver, but his grin assures me it was the right thing to say.

"I do think you're hot," he says. My whole body buzzes with delight.

"I think you're just okay," I say, and he tips his head back to laugh. The things I would do to his neck.

"I don't know if you really need any practice at this," he says, "you're a natural. I feel like I'm gonna get hustled or something." It's my turn to laugh.

"I haven't been on a date in years," I say. "I think I used to be okay at them. I mean, I never got any negative feedback"—this makes him smile—"but it's been a while. And I haven't really dated as, like, a guy."

"I was nervous about dating when I first came out, too," he says. "I was afraid of being too, like, fake, I guess? Like, when I dated as a girl I had to do a lot of fake laughing. I didn't want to make the people I was seeing do a lot of fake laughing on my behalf." I let this sink in for a moment. I could tell Mason was queer when I met him, but I wasn't sure what his particular flavor of gay was. The fact that he's also a trans guy makes me feel a little more comfortable in my chair, a little more settled at the table. A spot of warmth blooms in my chest.

"I think the biggest thing I'm afraid of is, like, having to explain myself all the time forever," I say finally. It's a more honest answer than I was expecting to give, but I want to be honest with Mason. He nods solemnly.

"Yeah. I mean, some people are always going to need an explanation. Which is basically neutral, but it can still be a headache." He tucks a lock of hair behind his ear, his dark eyes thoughtful. "But that kind of makes it even sweeter when you meet people who just see you. That sounds corny but it's also true. For example, I haven't had to explain myself to you," he says. He gives me a smile that's different from his flirty grin or his teasing smirk. This smile feels more genuine, and it's just a little sad. We both sit for a moment, thinking. A moment of silence passes, but it's a comfortable one.

"That's enough big thoughts for the evening," he says finally. "I can't help but notice you still haven't given me a compliment." He grins at me in a way that exposes one of his canines. A wave of want sweeps over me, leaving me giddy. But I take my time responding. I lean back and look him up and down. I can tell by a quirk of his eyebrows that he likes this; that he didn't expect it. My gaze finally lands on his hands—specifically his right thumb, which he's lazily dragging through the condensation on his water glass.

"You've got nice hands," I say. His grin widens and a blush creeps over his cheeks. Seeing him blush does something insane to my nervous system. Knowing that I'm the one who made him blush sends a bolt of heat to a place just below my stomach.

"That's what we call an end-of-the-night compliment," he says. "I didn't realize you were such a closer." I laugh and feel the bolt of heat move lower.

"Wait, what happens at the end of the night?" I ask with mock confusion.

"On a practice date? I walk you home. Maybe we shake hands or exchange a friendly hug," he says.

"What about on a real date?" I ask. He falls back against his chair and looks at me with a mix of thoughtfulness and surprise.

"I guess we'd have to go on a real date to find out," he says finally. He runs a hand through his hair.

"Too bad we're just practice dating," I reply.

His gaze turns a little more intense, but before he can say anything the waitress arrives with our food.

We spend the next few weeks going on practice dates. Slowly, I get more comfortable dating. Or practice dating. I'm starting to feel less like I'm trying to figure out who I am, and more like I know who I am and I'm letting that version of myself take the reins. I always used to think of myself as reserved. I preferred to fade into the background, to take up as little space as possible. But the new me is outgoing, maybe even charismatic. I say unbelievably flirty things to Mason without a second thought, and when he volleys back I accept his compliments without question.

I've felt strangely comfortable around Mason since the moment I met him, but now I'm starting to feel that kind of comfort around more things. I feel present and grounded and in my body in a way I haven't felt before. And around Mason, I feel extra present, extra grounded, extra-extra in my body. Everything that I feel 100 percent in other places, I feel 200 percent around him. I fall asleep thinking about his eyes and I have dreams about the line of his throat and all day I imagine what it would be like to suck on his neck tattoo.

These feelings make it both easier and harder to do our practice dates. Easier, because I want to flirt with him—harder, because I want to do a lot more. He takes me ice skating and we hold hands and I feel the heat of his skin even through both our gloves. He takes me for a drive in his extremely impractical little blue car and I'm embarrassed by how sexy I find his ability to drive stick. We go to the yearly winter carnival and we sit huddled together on the Ferris wheel, our bodies pressed together in a way that feels a little more than friendly. It's like living in a teen rom-com and I love it. I love getting to have this kind of simple, easy romance. Practice romance.

We're on the Ferris wheel when he tells me our next practice date will be our last. We're looking out over Cryptid Creek. It's cold out, and I'm wearing a jacket but there's a thin layer of frost stuck to the moss on my hands and face. I hope the frost is catching the light in a cool, sexy way. Mason is bundled up in his usual scarf mess. He's managed to wind the scarf around his head so that his face peeks out, and I know I'm really gone when I catch myself thinking how cute he looks like this.

"I think we need some kind of final exam, right?" he asks, interrupting my train of thought. "Otherwise we're just going on practice dates forever." That doesn't sound so bad to me, but

I don't say anything. I just nod. "I've been thinking that a good 'final exam' for this would be if you planned the last date," he says. I feel a little nervous. He's done such a good job planning our other dates, and I really want to give him back as much as he's given me.

"That makes sense," I say, still thinking it over. Although it's hard to think with his thigh pressed so firmly against mine.

"I'm not saying we can never hang out again," he says. I perk up at this. Is he going to ask me out for real?

"You'd want to hang out again?" I ask.

"Of course," he says. "You're my friend." I try to keep my face neutral after he says this. I *would* be happy to stay friends with Mason, after all. We get along and he's great company. I'd just prefer to have something a little . . . more.

"Yeah, you're my friend, too," I say. He gives me a half smile. The Ferris wheel is dotted in multicolored flashing lights, and I like watching his face light up red and green and blue. Each color exposes something a little new about his face. Something I didn't notice before.

At the end of the night, he walks me home. We hug. He says to call him when I finish planning the date. He says he's looking forward to it. He looks at me thoughtfully and runs his hand through his hair, and then leaves me outside my apartment.

How am I going to survive being just friends with him? How am I going to give up the dates and the flirting and those diabolical grins that send me into an absolute tailspin of longing? I'm not sure I can go through life with Mason right at my fingertips but never in my hand. I never knew I could want someone this badly. It's as if he's unlocked some new level of desire in me, and it hurts but it's so brutally sweet.

When I get inside my apartment, I vow to myself that I'm going to create a perfect, romantic date for him and then tell him how I really feel. At least then I'll know I tried. I'll know I did everything I could.

For our last date, I opt for something simple: dinner at my place. I spend the afternoon cooking vegetarian gumbo and making an "eating vegetarian gumbo with your crush before you tell them you like them" playlist. When the doorbell buzzes, my apartment is fragrant with the smell of dinner, my playlist is going quietly in the background, and my living room is as clean as it's going to get. I buzz Mason in and spend the time it takes for him to get upstairs fretting about my outfit choice (overalls and a hoodie). As soon as I open the door, though, my worries are forgotten.

He's carrying a small bouquet wrapped in brown paper and his eyelashes look even longer and darker than usual. He's wearing a light green T-shirt that's cropped just below his belly button. I try not to swoon when he smiles at me.

"You look nice," he says. There's a cigarette tucked behind his ear. I reach out and tap the cigarette. He grabs it from behind his ear. Our fingers brush for just a moment. "Oh, shit, I thought I lost that," he says when he sees what he's holding. "Sorry about that. I brought you flowers. And, uh, I guess you can have this too, if you want." He tucks the cigarette into the bouquet. I don't smoke, but I do want it. I'll take any piece of him I can get.

I accept the flowers and lead him into my apartment. He looks around, occasionally asking a question or complimenting something. He likes all my plants. He likes the music. I tell him it'll be a little bit longer before dinner's ready. (Actually, I finished cooking just before he got here, but I left the gumbo warming on the stove so we'd have time to talk.) We settle on the couch. Mason rests one arm on the back of the couch, his fingers a hairsbreadth from my shoulder. I try not to think about the proximity.

"So, have I been a good tutor?" he asks. His tone is casual, but his eyes search my face.

"You've been a great tutor," I reply. He's been more helpful than he could ever know. A few weeks ago I was feeling trapped—in my apartment, my life, my body. Mason has been like a door opening into the world. I'm not sure what it is about him that makes me feel like this. Really, it's everything. His easy smile, his straightforwardness, the instant intimacy that he's able to cultivate with almost anyone. He has this ability to slip right into someone's life as though he's always been there. He slipped right into mine.

"You were a pretty good student, too," he says. He reaches his hand a little closer to me and taps me on the shoulder. Heat radiates from where he touched me. I move a little closer to him.

"Does that mean I'm gonna pass the final exam?" I ask. He

grins and I catch a glimpse of his canines.

"I have to admit something," he says, leaning in conspiratorially. I lean in too, my heart pounding. Our faces are so close that I can see a tiny scar I hadn't noticed before on his upper lip. "I never came up with any rules for the practice dates," he whispers. Before I can say anything else, he whispers again: "I have to admit something else." I raise my eyebrows, waiting. "I don't think practice dates are a real thing." I laugh again, but now I'm a little confused.

"What do you mean they're not real?" I ask. He bites his bottom lip and drums his fingers on his knee, thinking.

"I think they're just, like, a trope in romance novels. I don't think people go on 'practice dates' in real life," he says. I furrow my eyebrows.

"Then what have we been doing?" I ask. He bites his lip again, this time like he's trying to hide a smile.

"I think we've just been dating," he says finally. My face goes hot and my heart races. I laugh and my laugh sounds breathy and a little too loud. I've been dating Mason? I mean, I know I've been "dating" Mason, but I didn't realize I'd been *dating* him. If I'd known we were going out for real, I would've made a move a long time ago. Maybe immediately. Maybe the second I saw him.

But I think back to how I felt when I first saw Mason—the place I was in when I first met him. The idea that that version of me could have made a move on him is silly. I was so closed up, so uncertain of myself. Watching Mason's body move through space changed the way my body moved through space. Without him, I think I'd still be an anxious mess trapped in my apartment.

Then again, isn't that anxious mess the version of me who agreed to the practice dates? Who saw Mason and trusted him and knew that he would be good for me? I feel a sudden wave of empathy for my past self. I had spent the last few weeks slowly slipping into my body, learning about what I liked and didn't like. Seeing Mason but also seeing myself, maybe for the first time. It's true that Mason was the catalyst for a lot of personal growth, but it's me who did the work of growing. Or maybe it's something we did together.

Mason is still watching me, an uncertain look in his dark eyes. I'm so happy to be here with him. I smile.

"If we're dating, then I guess it's okay if I do this," I say, and I do the thing I've been wanting to do since the moment I saw him: I kiss him. And he kisses me back. And the kiss is hot and hard and deep, and I'm running my hands through his perfect hair and his fingertips are on my neck. When we finally break apart, I've lost all sense of time. I open my eyes and look at him. His lips are bitten red and his hair is messy and his face is smeared with wet from my mossy skin. He looks impossibly, impossibly hot. He blinks at me, his eyes hooded, his expression both focused and lost. I've never been more turned on in my life.

I reach forward and pull at the hem of his shirt. He takes it off immediately, like I gave him a command. He locks eyes with me as if asking for more. I run a finger along the waist of his pants and he quickly stands and takes them off too, then just as fast he's sitting in front of me again. His gaze is dark, desperate, full of want and waiting. I inhale the knowledge that he wants me as much as I want him. It leaves me feeling dizzy. I run a finger down his arm and watch a trail of goosebumps form in its wake. I barely need to lean in before we're kissing again, his tongue in my mouth, his hands undoing the straps of my overalls, pulling off my hoodie.

I lay back and instantly he's straddling me, kissing me even harder than before. I revel in the feeling of his body on top of mine, in the frantic but precise movement of his hands. The way he touches me—it's like he already knows my body. Like we've done this before. I push his head lower. He glances up and gives me his most diabolical grin, then enthusiastically complies.

By the time we're done, his whole body is slick with damp, and there are bits of moss and lichen in his hair and stuck to his chin. I feel like someone scooped out all my organs and put them back in upside down, but in a good way. I'm hot and shivery and exultant and alive. My overalls are on the floor. He's sitting on the couch by my feet, running his hands along my legs.

"Cleo was right," I say after a few minutes of contented silence, "you really are a slut." Mason bursts out laughing at this, the kind of laugh that makes him tip his head back and expose his tattoo. I bite my lip, remembering how his neck tasted on my tongue.

"I'm willing to tutor you in that, too," he says, "although I don't think you need any help." He winks at me and my stomach flips over. I didn't think anything could be this easy. Being with him feels like I've always been with him. As I sit, my body buzzing with the memory of Mason's fingers and mouth and tongue, my brain pleasantly foggy, I'm suddenly struck by the feeling of being completely in my body. I'm happier than I've been in a long, long time. I'm here.

RIPPLE

I've been looking for signs of Beth even more today. Looking for signs is difficult. Every day I see so many beautiful things, and every day I think so often of Beth. But I don't count every beautiful thing as a sign from her. It's only certain things: sandhill cranes, sudden fog, a full moon you can see during the day. It's cloudy today and the season is late for cranes. All I have of her today is her kayak. I push a paddle through the dark water and watch the ripples swirl.

Beth always loved paddling around this lake in her shitty little kayak. She's been gone for two years now. I thought it was finally time to go out on the water myself. I wasn't planning on taking her boat out today, I just woke up this morning and knew I had to do it, knew it somewhere under my skin, inside my bones. A lot of my time now is spent trying to be with her. But a lot of my time when she was alive was spent trying to be with her, too. Some things don't totally change.

I drag the dented one-seater kayak from the bed of my truck to the edge of the water. When I get in, it takes me a minute to get used to the gentle sway and lap of the water. But once I start paddling, I settle in quickly.

Fall is coming. Today was the first day I noticed the sun coming up a little later. The lake had a low rind of fog. In my sketch from this day last year, there was a family of ducks sitting in the reeds. I haven't seen those ducks in a few weeks. If I wasn't paying much attention, I might think the lake looked identical every day. But since I've been coming to the lake every morning to draw and think and watch the seasons change, I've gotten used to its subtle gradations in color, the lightest of its blues and the deepest of its greens. The frothy gray that comes over it when there's a storm. The days when the light skips over the water's surface and the days when it gets absorbed into the depths. The plants that grow on the banks at different times of year, the birds that visit and nest and eat.

Beth had been an avid bird-watcher since she was a kid. Her favorites were sandhill cranes, but she also had a soft spot for loons and herons, terns and kingfishers. She loved waterbirds. She wanted to build a house by the lake someday, when we were old and tired of living in town. She made do with coming here every day and watching the birds from her kayak. She measured the year in migrations.

Wisps of mist curl around my oars. Near shore, seaweed reaches from the bottom of the lake toward the surface. I've seen the water from shore so many times, but I've never been in it like this. Never floated over the rocks, then the kelp, then the deep dark center of the lake. What's at the bottom of this lake, under all this dark water? Is it a heart? Or a stomach? I sit and float and tiny waves lap against Beth's kayak.

I wonder what she used to think about when she came out here. I was never a morning person when Beth was alive, but I don't sleep much anymore. I might as well get up early if I'm awake anyway. Beth used to pester me about waking up earlier, but I think deep down she liked having her mornings to herself. Sometimes she would live a whole day before I even woke up. When we first got married, this bothered me. Beth could be distant, private, reserved. She would slip out of the house without me noticing, forget her phone at home, take too long to call me back. I joked that being married to her was more like having a cat than a wife. But she was also thoughtful and caring and sometimes it seemed like she could read my mind. She would come home from her private wanderings with a bouquet of wildflowers in my favorite color or a fallen bird nest for me to draw. She saw me so clearly.

From the middle of the lake, the shore looks different. The tall grass looks lighter, the trees smaller. The alders are just starting to turn yellow—barely yellow, a kind of green-yellow that's most noticeable when the leaves move in the breeze. The water looks different, too. So dark it's almost a solid object. So green it's almost alive.

I look over the edge of the kayak and see a school of tiny fish slipping through the water, like liquid silver flashing near the surface. I'm watching the fish when I notice a dark shape passing deep under my boat. It's too large to be a seal or an otter—it's easily two or three times the size of the kayak. I know before I even hear the loud exhale behind me, before I turn and see her head and neck rising up out of the water, that it's Nessie. The lake monster.

Her head breaks through the surface tension, her long, smooth neck sparkling in the light, the tall hump of her back like a wet stone revealed at low tide. I wait for the ripples from her emergence to gently lick my boat. I've never talked to her before, but I've drawn her many times. I was fascinated by her beauty, by her distance. I've never been this close to her before. I imagine that if I touched her, her skin would be cool and smooth as the lake itself.

For a moment, neither of us does anything. We just stare at each other. Her eyes are huge and dark, her eyelids heavy. I can see individual drops of water running down her neck.

Suddenly, a voice is in my head. Low and fluid, like a slow-moving river. It seems to slither from my conscious mind to my subconscious and back again. I shiver at the sensation.

I know you, says the voice. Nessie's gaze is steady. *You're the artist*, she says. I'm so surprised that I almost can't respond.

"I'm Bridget," I finally manage.

Bridget the artist, she says. I feel her running my name over in her mind. *You're normally on the shore.*

"I wanted to see what the shore would look like from out here," I say. She nods thoughtfully. She swims a little closer to me.

I recognize this boat, she says. My heart crawls into my throat. I hadn't considered that she had seen Beth out here. I hadn't considered that maybe they'd even talked, like we were talking now.

I steel myself for Nessie to mention my wife, but she doesn't say anything else. She just angles her head to look at me better with one of her big, dark eyes. We float together silently. I'm grateful for the silence. A breeze blows across the water and I watch ripples drag across the surface.

You said you wanted to see the shore from the lake, she says after a minute has passed. *Can you show me the lake from the shore?* she asks, and nods at my sketchbook. I don't usually show people my art. But I would give Nessie whatever she wanted. I put my sketchbook in my lap and flip through the pages. She swims even closer to the boat and puts her head over my shoulder to look. I try to keep my focus on my drawings. This close, she smells sharp and brackish, as salty as tidal mud.

I show her a drawing from last week, when the sun cut across the water in crisp shafts of light and the sky was full of geese. I flip to a page from last winter, when the lake was ringed with ice and the shore was bare and quiet. When I show her a sketch from summer, she sighs.

I always love summer, she says. I turn to look at her and see her eyes moving thoughtfully over the sketch, with its lush trees and overgrown shoreline. *It always feels the most alive.*

"Does it ever feel too alive to you?" I ask. She tilts her neck to look at me. "Like, too rich, I guess? Sometimes I feel like I'm drowning in summer." I'm quiet. I don't know what made me say this to her.

She looks down into the water just as another school of tiny fish swims past. *In your drawing, everything is leaning in to this lake. Everything is growing toward the water. There's a sense of desperation.* She nods at my summer sketch. She's right that all the plants seemed to be reaching for the middle of the lake, pointing to their life source. *From out here, it doesn't feel like that. That need is—not gone, but less apparent. It doesn't feel like need, it just feels like presence.* She blinks at me slowly.

I look away from her. She's right that from here, the season feels different. From shore, autumn was low light and yellow; an ebbing; a quieting. From here I can still see all that, but the overwhelming sensation is one of remove, like the world is taking a step back from this place. Already the trees seem to have fewer leaves than they did when I arrived.

I glance at Nessie to find that she's still watching me. We float gently beside each other for a moment, neither of us saying anything. I think about how Beth had never mentioned Nessie. I think about how much of her life would always be a mystery to me. How much of her life would be a mystery to me even if she were still alive.

"It's nice to sit with you," I say. I paddle the kayak a little so I'm facing Nessie. She nods.

I don't get to see many people this time of year, she says. In my head, her voice feels heavy. A cold wind blows across the water.

"Would it be okay if I came back tomorrow?" I ask. She swims a little closer, and I'm struck again by how long her neck is, how the water droplets on her skin catch the light.

Please, she says. Then she sinks back under the water and is gone. She disappears so quickly and quietly that the whole exchange feels like a dream. I'm alone, sitting in Beth's boat, far from shore.

I wake up before dawn the next day. It's been a long time since I had something to look forward to, and the feeling of anticipation is strange. I put on a flannel that Beth and I had shared and drink my coffee too quickly. When I can't wait anymore, when the stars are just starting to fade into the pink sky, I pull on my old quilted jacket and drive to the lake.

I don't see Nessie anywhere. There is only still, green water and the sunrise sky. I get the kayak in the water and paddle to the middle of the lake. Almost as soon as I stop paddling, Nessie appears beside me. She looks slightly golden in the morning light. A thin trail of steam rises from her head into the cool air.

"I want to show you something," I say before I can lose my nerve. She swims closer to me, her fins moving lazily in the water. I pull out a sketchbook, different from the one I showed her yesterday. Once again, she peers over my shoulder, so close that a few drops of water fall from her head onto my boots. I open the book.

Oh, she breathes as I flip past a drawing of her neck curving out of the water. I turn the page and it's another drawing of Nessie, this time in the semidark, looking off toward the rising sun. It's strange showing Nessie these drawings. Part of me is worried that she'll be disgusted by my voyeurism, and part of me wants to see how she'll react to knowing I was watching. I shiver.

I can feel only Nessie's breath warm on my neck, can smell only the seaweedy scent of her skin. I feel like the pit of my stomach has dropped away. A thrill runs through my body and I am suddenly overcome by a sensation I haven't felt in years—desire. A longing so deep I can feel it in my teeth. I turn to look at her and find my own face reflected back at me in her watery eye. My reflection looks strange and warped. In the middle of my face, her pupil hangs steadily, focused on me.

I like the way you draw me, she says. A fish jumps a few yards away. There is a quick flash of silver and splash, and then it's gone.

"I should be getting back," I say. I am suddenly overwhelmed. I turn and Nessie is already a few feet away. She moves silently, gracefully. She barely creates any ripples. More like a beam of light than a physical creature.

Can I see you tomorrow? she asks. I nod. She begins to sink back into the lake. *I'll see you then,* she says, and she is gone. I shake myself, then paddle back to shore. Almost as soon as I get out of the boat, I throw up. I spit into the mud, hoping Nessie isn't watching. I haven't been that near to anyone since Beth. It feels like a betrayal. I keep reminding myself that Beth isn't here, that she'll never be here again. The taste of vomit is sharp on my tongue.

Lightheaded, I walk back to my truck and drive home. I sleep until dusk. When I wake up, I make tea and drink it out of Beth's mug.

Beth and I were together for ten years, married for three. The details of our relationship are worn smooth by now. I think about them all the time—the way we met, our first date, when I told her I was a woman, the day we got married. Remembering these moments releases a familiar flavor, as simple as water.

I am overwhelmed, suddenly, by a memory I don't often think of. One I've tried to keep safe from erosion. The first time we slept together after I started taking estrogen.

Beth always gave me my shots. I was too nervous to do it myself and she had steady hands. She'd count to three and stab me just below the hip.

We hadn't had sex in a while. I'd been too nervous, and she understood. For some reason, though, on this day, when the needle pricked my skin and I looked in the mirror at her looking so seriously at her task and I saw myself standing beside her, naked and wet from a shower, I suddenly wanted her beyond words.

I watched her finish my shot and dispose of the needle. I put a finger under her chin and lifted her face to look at mine. She could always tell what I was thinking, and this time was no different. Her hands slid up and down my legs, warming my skin. I ran a hand through her eternally tangled blond hair and bent to kiss her. She was gentle with me as she was always gentle with me. She led me out of the bathroom and over to the bed.

"Is this okay?" she asked. Or, she probably asked it—she asked so many times that day if what she was doing was okay. We kissed and I remember these kisses as distinct from all others before or after. We moved slower, held each moment for longer. Her teeth dragged against my lower lip and her spit tasted like weed and dark chocolate. I could have lived on just her spit. When she laid me out on the bed and started eating me out, I cried. She stopped what she was doing and lay down next to me.

"What's wrong?" she asked. I wasn't sure how to explain what I was feeling. I'd never felt so embodied before, so fully in my body. I shook my head and ran a hand down her jaw.

"I just like being with you," I said. She smiled. She had a smile that completely disarmed me. No matter how many times I saw it, it left me out of breath.

"I like being with you too," she said. I always felt lucky to have her. I kissed her. "Can I finish what I was doing?" she asked.

"If it's okay, I'd rather fuck you," I said. Her pupils grew large and her eyelids grew heavy. When she said yes, her voice was deep and throaty in a way that turned me on more than was reasonable.

Normally when we fucked, there was a sense of desperation, a series of moans asked and answered in quick succession. This time I moved slowly and she responded with the same languid energy. We giggled at the newness of some things, inhaled into the familiarity of others. It wasn't like sleeping together for the first time, but it wasn't like every other time we'd slept together, either. We were both more attentive and more likely to linger. After we finished, we fell asleep, tangled together, breathing matched.

What Beth and I had was singular. I miss her and I miss the person I was with her and I miss the living thing of our relationship. I know she would want me to be happy even after she was gone, but I also know she'd understand the unbearable weight of mourning. She'd understand that it's hard to start a new life, hard to find easy happiness when you're always exhausted.

But today has felt a little different than every other day had felt since I lost Beth. It's nice to have a respite from the monotony of grief. I hope Beth and Nessie did meet. I hope someday Nessie can tell me what they talked about during Beth's early morning trips to the lake. I hope to see Nessie again tomorrow. It still won't be easy, but maybe tomorrow if she touches me I won't throw up. That's something I can look forward to.

Nessie is waiting for me near the shoreline as soon as I get out of my car. The sky is overcast and she is the exact silvery-gray as the clouds. Once I have the boat in the water, I paddle over to her. I'd debated this morning about whether or not I would come to the lake. I was afraid of seeing Nessie, but also afraid of not seeing her. The lure of familiarity versus the lure of something new. The paralyzing fear of both. In the end, though, I decided that this was what I wanted. I wanted to take the kayak to the lake, and paddle out into the dark water, and talk to the beautiful lake monster who said I was an artist.

What are you going to draw today? she asks. I pull my sketchbook out of my backpack and flip to the next blank page.

"I was wondering, actually, if I could draw you today?" I hold my breath, nervous for her to say no. Her eyes grow round.

I'd love that, she says. I exhale.

"I've never gotten to draw you from this close before," I explain.

How would you like to draw me? she asks.

"Maybe you could go over here by the seagrass? That might be a nice background." I point to an area not far from me where the pale green seagrass sways in the water. She swims to where I'm pointing. "Yeah, that's good. And maybe you could tilt your head a little, like—yeah, like that. Perfect." I start drawing.

My pencil traces the lines of her neck and I imagine running my hand along her skin. I sketch her back and imagine what she would feel like underneath me. The breeze picks up and her briney scent fills my lungs. I imagine that if I were to taste her, she would be tart and earthy with a tang of decay. I swallow and keep drawing.

How long have you been drawing? she asks.

"It's just something I've always done," I say. "I tried to make a job out of it for a little while, but that sucked. Now I just work at the coffee shop." What I don't say: I used to have a nine-to-five but I used up all my vacation days after Beth died and I got laid off. The coffee shop gig was more a pity hire from Mothman than anything else. I wasn't hugely successful as a barista, although I could do decent latte art.

"Do you like doing art?" I ask. "Or—can you do any art in the water?" She smiles.

Sometimes I chase the fish into one place so I can see what they look like somewhere else. Sometimes I sing. Her face changes and she looks sad. I sketch the downcast look in her eyes.

"My wife used to sing a lot," I say, not looking up from my drawing. She is quiet for a moment.

Was she good at it? she asks finally. I snort.

"She was an awful singer. And it was honestly really annoying. It's something I never really warmed up to when she was around. I miss it now, though," I say.

Another quiet moment passes. *It's hard to lose people,* she says. *Sometimes I think you can't experience loss without going insane.* A laugh I wasn't expecting bursts out of me. It echoes awkwardly through the air.

"Sorry," I say, "I hadn't thought of it like that. But you're right." I shade in the clouds. The only sound is my pencil scratching against the paper and the quiet lapping of water against the side of my boat. "Who did you lose?" I ask finally. Nessie looks up at me.

Oh, I lost everyone, she says. The look in her eyes is sad and distant. *There used to be a lot of us. A long, long time ago. Now there's only me.* I put down my notebook.

"Shit," I say. There's no good way to respond to someone's loss, which is partly why I usually avoid talking about Beth. "Sorry. I don't know what to say," I admit. The corners of her mouth turn up in an impression of a smile.

There's nothing to say, she tells me. *But you know what it's like. Being alone, I mean.* I sigh and pick my sketchbook back up.

"Can I ask you something that might sound a little cold?" I ask. She nods. "How did you get through that?" She considers my question.

A version of me didn't. There are a lot of versions of me that stopped existing when it happened. You probably had the same experience. She's right. I often think that the version of me that was with Beth had died just as completely as Beth had. I'm something different now. *I don't know if anyone really survives a loss like that.* We both float quietly for a moment, the silence comfortable. *Today is a nice day, though. It's nice that you're drawing me.*

"Yeah, it is nice," I say. "I'm finished now if you want to see." I hold out the drawing and she glides over to me. From this close, I can see individual drops of water shining on her brow. She towers over me, her reflection shimmering in the water at my side. She looks at the drawing and at me and then smiles. I smile back. The air is cool and the clouds still hang silver in the sky. The water is gray-green. The ducks are still gone. Somewhere in the distance, I hear a crane crying.

NIGHT SHIFT

The door was made of dark, heavy wood and it stood before me like something alive. In the middle was an ornately carved silver knocker in the shape of a magpie. Under a layer of grime, I could just make out a pair of ruby eyes peering out at me from the silver face.

I had long admired this house—its warped windows and uneven shingles, the hedges that curled unkempt around the edge of the property. The house seemed like it had grown up out of the soil, its shape wrong and bent in a way that felt organic: a tree that grew at a strange angle. I knew the woman who lived here was called Flatwoods and that she rarely left this house, but I knew little else about her. No one else in town seemed to know much about her either.

The porch below me creaked under my weight as I shifted nervously, trying to get up the courage to knock. My backpack straps dug into my shoulders. The bag was full of supplies: crys-

Flatwoods

tals and herbs, tarot cards and a Ouija board, lots of salt, silver spoons. My family was one of the first human families to move to Cryptid Creek two generations ago, and we'd been in the psychic business for as long as anyone could remember. People called on us for all kinds of reasons, from fortune-telling to energy cleansing, but we didn't get too many jobs like this. In my life, we'd only handled one or two other hauntings. I'd never seen a ghost before.

Last night I dreamed I was in a cave, dark and dripping, somewhere deep underground. I'd slowly become aware that there was a beautiful woman in the cave with me, her hair so long and shining that it seemed to cast its own light. I knew she needed something, but she didn't speak. She only looked at me and slowly raised her right hand until she was pointing at me. It was then that I realized her hands were strange and gnarled, her fingers too long and her nails long and thick as claws. I felt afraid but I also felt something else. Sad, I think. Like the sadness that comes from being alone for too long. It was the sadness, not the fear, that woke me up.

I shook myself out of the memory of the dream. I'd been standing on the porch for too long, an uncomfortable amount of time. I steeled myself and lifted the knocker. The sound of metal on wood split the evening air and echoed through the house. Everything was quiet for a moment. I thought about knocking again when I became aware of a strange sound deep within the house. It was so faint that at first I thought it was just my ears ringing. But the sound got louder, became more defined. A mechanical whirring. When the sound reached its zenith, the front door swung open.

It took me a moment to make sense of what I was seeing. An enormous woman, at least seven feet tall, was standing in the open doorway. She was wearing an old-fashioned dress with a wide skirt. She had on a tear-shaped headdress that billowed around the back of her head and came to a point on top. She looked at me with glowing yellow eyes, huge and round. They were so bright I could feel their warmth on my face. But strangest of all was the fact that all of her—from her dress to her hands to her face to her headdress—seemed to be made of solid metal. A dark, shiny metal, so polished that the last rays of sunlight seemed to slip over it like water. She was, put simply, stunning.

"You're Theodora?" she asked. Her voice sounded scratchy, staticky, like a radio station just barely in range. The sound emanated from somewhere in her chest. I startled to hear my name in her voice.

"Just Theo is fine," I said. Her neck made a mechanical clicking sound as she looked me up and down.

"You seem a little young," she said. I bristled.

"I'm almost thirty," I said. She crossed her arms over her chest and the movement caused all kinds of little tapping sounds throughout her body.

"Are you sure you'll be able to help me?" she asked. Her voice had a condescending tone. I bristled more. I narrowed my eyes and tried to keep my tone civil.

"I've been doing this my whole life," I said. She looked at

me for another moment and finally shrugged, although I got the sense she wasn't convinced.

"I guess you might as well give it a shot," she said, and without another word she turned and moved back into the house. I followed, equally irritated and curious.

Inside the house, Flatwoods glided over the scuffed parquet floors. She was hovering an inch or two above the floor. The whole house was dark, lit only by an occasional candle or whatever light could filter in through the dirty windows. What few lamps there were all seemed broken or burnt out. Flatwoods's eyes guided the way like twin flashlights, illuminating the uneven stairs in the grand staircase, the haphazardly placed rugs that dampened sound, the statues half hidden in shadowy corners. She said very little as she guided me around, mostly noting which room we were in.

Upstairs, she showed me where I'd be staying—ghost hunting can take days, and it's better to sleep at the site of the haunting. The room was simple: a small fireplace, a bed, a desk, and a dresser. The most notable thing was how clean it was—unlike the rest of the house, it wasn't cobwebbed and dingy. It was as though Flatwoods had spent some time cleaning it up before I arrived. I glanced at her as I took in the room, but she didn't say anything about it.

"There's a bathroom next door, and my room is across the hall," she said. Then, looking down at me: "I expect you to be clean and quiet while you're residing here." I raised an eyebrow. She really did think I was a child.

"Yeah, I think I can manage that," I said after a beat. She nodded, her neck squeaking like it needed to be oiled. I put my backpack down and pulled out a notebook and pen.

"Could you tell me a little more about this haunting?" I asked, clicking my pen. I wanted her to see that I was professional and ready to work. She tilted her head.

"I already told you everything on the phone. Well, not you, but your—what, business partner?" she asked. I cleared my throat.

"That was my mom," I said, embarrassed. I would never beat the idiot child allegations at this rate. Flatwoods was giving me a look like she agreed. "We're a family business—" I started to explain, but Flatwoods began talking over me.

"As I told your mother"—I winced—"I don't know if this is a ghost or poltergeist or what have you. I'm not particularly familiar with spiritual phenomena. The house was empty when I moved in, so I can't inquire with the previous owners about their experiences, although I've been here over a year with no notable occurrences." I scribbled in my notebook as she spoke. Most of this I already knew, but I thought it would be useful to hear it directly from her.

"So the weird stuff—er, the phenomena, has only been happening for how long?" I asked.

She crossed her arms over her chest and stuck one hip out a bit, striking an impressively bitchy pose. "About a month," she said. "It's generally small things—objects being rearranged when I leave a room, candles suddenly flaring up, footsteps in the attic. But it's becoming tiresome and I'd like it fixed," she said. She peered over the top of my notebook to look at what I was writing.

"How are you ever going to read those notes? Your handwriting is a mess," she said. I snapped the notebook closed.

"It sounds like you have a pretty straightforward haunting," I said, choosing not to respond to her handwriting comment. "I should be able to sort it out in a day or two." Flatwoods nodded, but her posture remained defensive. The glow from her yellow eyes was warm on my face, and I was struck again by how singular her appearance was. Then she spoke and my moment of warmth vanished.

"And you said you've done this before?" she asked. It took everything in me not to roll my eyes. I gave her a forced smile instead.

"Yes. Like I said, I've been doing this my whole life. In fact, everyone in my family has been doing this their whole lives. The Song family is—" She waved her hand to dismiss me.

"But you've personally done this exact task before? On your own?" she asked. I breathed out very slowly through my nose, trying to collect myself. My jaw was clenched tight in annoyance.

"I am a professional and a grown-up." I realized too late that it didn't make me sound very adult to defend my adulthood. The truth was that I hadn't done this *exact* task before. I didn't want Flatwoods to know that, though. Besides, I knew I could handle this whether I'd done it before or not. We both stood for a moment, staring at each other.

"If you say so," she said finally. I chose not to respond. "You're welcome to begin your investigation tonight." She turned and glided across the hall toward her room. I put my backpack on the bed and began unpacking.

"Theo?" I jumped when I heard her crackly voice from her doorway across the hall. "I suppose the room is to your liking?" she asked. I stared at her. Although her words were as snobby as usual, something in her tone seemed earnest. Her hand rested on her doorframe, her long metal fingers tapping the wood nervously. Her head was tilted at an angle that made her look unguarded.

"Oh, uh, yeah. It's really nice," I said honestly. I gave her a nervous half smile and realized that for some reason I was blushing. She just nodded and whirred into her room. I shook my head when I heard her door close. I didn't feel like unpacking all of that just now. I took my old tarot deck and some chalk out of my bag. I tried not to think about my dream, about the beautiful woman and the pit of sadness she planted in me.

Catching whatever was in the house ended up being harder than I thought. I'd expected this job to last a day or two at most, but four days later I was still chasing shadows and listening for whispers. Flatwoods was not impressed by this, and took every possible opportunity to question my credentials. Unfortunately our working hours were the same (nighttime), so I had to see a lot of her. Sometimes I could swear she was following me around just to annoy me.

On the fourth night, I was setting up for a séance on the floor of the parlor. I took my time arranging little bundles of herbs (rosemary for protection, lavender to increase my psychic abilities), a pinch pot of salt, a cinnamon stick, an orange sliced in half, a handful of quartz crystals, and seven white votive candles in a circle on the ground. Everything had its particular place in the circle; the salt on my left, the cinnamon stick to my right, one half of the orange in front of me and the other at the opposite end of the circle, both cut side up. I placed the herbs and quartz between the candles. When everything was set up, I went to the kitchen to brew some tea.

My mother hammered it into me that I always needed to be polite to the powers that be, to offer them something, even if it was something small. She would sometimes make a full meal as an offering if she was doing a particularly complicated ritual. I liked to start with a cup of my favorite black tea and work from there.

I poured water into a heavy, old kettle and set it on the stove. The kitchen was one of the few rooms with a working light, although it did little to make the room seem welcoming. The old brick wall was scorched in several places, the paint chipping where there was paint. The overhead light mostly served to highlight the shadowy corners and the awkward way the back door sat in its frame.

I was lost in thought, mentally double-checking that I had set up the séance correctly, trying to decide if I should use tarot cards or a Ouija board to communicate. It took me a few minutes to realize Flatwoods was standing in the entrance of the kitchen, quietly watching me.

I startled when I finally saw her. I was still getting used to her big yellow eyes peering out at me from her strange, dark headdress. She was so often making noise—whirring, clicking, ticking, tapping—that I didn't realize how utterly silent she could sometimes be. I put a hand on my chest to calm myself down.

"Taking a break?" she asked. Such a simple question, yet her tone was so judgmental. I felt a ripple of annoyance.

"Nope," I said, sounding annoyed even to myself, "it's all part of the process." A whirring as Flatwoods came closer. She stopped just a few steps from me. She surveyed me intensely, like she was inspecting me. Like she was looking for some visible sign of failure or wrongdoing.

"Have you made any progress yet?" she asked.

"It's hard to say," I replied, picking at my nail polish. "The psychic thing is more of an art than a science." The truth was, I couldn't believe how badly I'd been doing. Normally I loved my job. I loved spending time setting up a séance, I loved the way my worn-out tarot deck felt in my hands, I loved the little spark I felt in my stomach when I knew I was communing with something bigger than myself. But since I'd been in Flatwoods's house, I'd felt completely incompetent. I was grasping around in the dark and only finding more void. Flatwoods was still looking at me, her eyes so bright that I could see them even when I blinked.

"No progress and it's been four days," she said, nodding to

herself. "And yet when you came here, you said it would take a day or two." She nodded again, as if confirming something she'd been suspecting. Heat flared in my chest.

"Like I said, it's more of an art than a science," I said through gritted teeth.

"I find that good art is very precise. Do you think there's a better way to do this?" she asked. I was getting to the end of my rope with her. The picking, the doubt, the constant corrections. I couldn't say anything to her without being scrutinized. And the worst part was that apparently she was right to doubt me. It's not like I'd made any headway in the last four days.

"I'm doing things the best way I know how," I said.

"Maybe someone else knows a better way. Maybe if you called your mother—" This immediately pushed me over the edge.

"I know how to do my fucking job," I spat. I could feel my face getting red. She stood up straighter, her body squeaking a little with the movement.

"That's not very professional," she said. I dug my nails into my palms.

"Maybe I'd act like a professional if you treated me like one," I said. I tried to keep my voice level but I could hear anger burning into my words. I opened my mouth to say something else, but that's when I noticed something strange. A creeping darkness seeping into the room.

At first I thought I was seeing things, but then a candle by the back door went out. The light overhead flickered and switched off. Flatwoods and I both watched a wave of darkness moving into the room. We both backed up as it approached. I felt a buzz of fear in some deep, primal part of my brain. The temperature in the kitchen was dropping.

"What is this?" asked Flatwoods.

"I don't know," I admitted. The shadow had spread to over half the room and it kept growing. Like water trickling through a broken pipe.

Then, a sound. A scraping sound. Nails drawn across glass, scratching and skittering somewhere nearby. Very nearby. It was coming from the back door.

I could hear each individual claw scraping the glass. The sound was horrible, shrill and screeching, something I could feel at the base of my skull. All I could think was that whatever was making this noise couldn't be allowed to come inside. We were only safe while it was out there.

The back door banged open. I didn't think, I just turned on my heel and ran as fast as I could. I could hear Flatwoods whirring right beside me. We raced into the sitting room and I slammed the door behind us. There was a bang as something large collided with the closed door. I took a step back and tripped over Flatwoods. We fell to the ground in a heap. The doorknob rattled violently like someone outside was shaking it. My vision tunneled until all I could see was the shaking doorknob. The room was freezing.

Then, just as suddenly as everything started, it stopped. The knob went still, there was no sound from the hallway. The temperature slowly returned to normal.

"I think it's gone," I said after a few minutes had passed in silence. I turned and realized that I was basically sitting in Flatwoods's lap. Her eyes locked on mine. Her metal body was warm against me. My heart beat so fast that I felt like it was trembling in my chest. My breath was quick and ragged. Without thinking, I ran a thumb down her cheek, feeling a little slick of grease, noticing a slight mineral smell this close to her.

Flatwoods reached out and rested a hand over mine. I stilled. Her fingers were long and dark, with ridges where her joints would be. They came to points at the end as if she had claws.

"Sorry," I said. She didn't respond. Her eyes were so big and bright, and the teardrop shape of her headdress was so otherworldly. Looking at Flatwoods was like looking at a piece of art. Except her lines were preternaturally smooth, the round slope of her chin more perfect than human hands could have made.

My brain felt shattered, my nerves shot. Her eyes were blinding from this close. I took a deep breath.

"I should go," I whispered. Slowly, she nodded. I slid off her lap and she stood with a series of hisses and pops. She took my hand and pulled me up like I weighed nothing. I hadn't realized how strong she was. We stood for another moment, our hands still clasped together. I became aware of a distant screech. The tea kettle whistling in the kitchen. The sound pulled me out of my trance. I let go of Flatwoods's hand and went to the kitchen door.

At the stove, I poured my tea leaves into a teapot and waited for them to steep.

Night Shift

I avoided Flatwoods for most of the next day and night. I wasn't sure what had happened between us when we were trapped in that room—I wasn't sure if anything had happened between us at all—but I didn't feel like unpacking it. I had enough going on. It was around midnight that I heard the sound. A clanging—loud and irregular, almost unearthly. I sat up from my desk, where I'd been taking case notes. My room looked strange when it was only lit by moonlight, as if everything was shifted a few inches from where it usually was. The shadows were eerie and warped. The sound grew louder. It was like a tuning fork being struck on the hull of a ship. A wave of goosebumps swept over me.

As a psychic, I'd learned to trust the goosebumps, the hair standing up at the back of my neck, the automatic quickening of breath. These weren't just involuntary reactions—they were signs. My body was pointing me in the direction of the haunting. I got out of bed.

There was a light on in the kitchen. The noise was definitely coming from in there. I tiptoed down the stairs and peered into the kitchen, every muscle in my body tense. But when I looked around, I saw the source of the noise: It was Flatwoods, sitting alone at the kitchen table with a game of solitaire spread out in front of her. I let out a breath.

"Hey," I said. Flatwoods jumped and turned to face me. The clanging stopped. "Sorry to scare you," I said, stepping into the kitchen. Her eyes were lit up particularly bright.

"What are you doing down here?" she said finally.

"I heard a weird noise. I was just checking it out," I said.

"I didn't hear anything," she said, "but feel free to look around." She went back to her cards. I looked at her, waiting to see if she was joking. The noise had clearly come from her—what did she mean she hadn't heard anything?

"I think you were actually making the sound I heard," I said. Flatwoods looked at me again. She sat up a little straighter.

"I think I would've noticed if I was making an odd sound," she said. I thought about pushing the issue, but I was tired. I decided to try a different tack.

"What are you playing?" I asked, walking over to the table. She turned back to her game.

"Just solitaire," she said. I stood with one hand on the back of her chair and one hand on the edge of the table and watched her play. The room was quiet except for the little clicks and taps that came from inside Flatwoods. "Could you not stand there?" she said after a minute. She didn't look up from her game. "You're looming," she said, and flipped over a new card.

"Oh, sorry," I said. I sat down in the chair next to her. "Do you play a lot of cards?" I asked.

"I do," she said. "Card games are very simple. They're all just patterns. Kind of like machines, in a way." She laid down her last card and sighed. "But they can still be so complicated." She swept the cards off the table and began shuffling them. Her long, metal fingers were much more dexterous than I would've expected. Another quiet moment passed as I watched her shuffle the cards. There was a gas lamp on the table, and the light flickered across Flatwoods's shiny carapace.

"I can teach you a game, if you'd like," she said. I looked up, surprised. This was the first friendly thing she'd said to me since I got here. I could only nod. She dealt us each a hand and explained the rules. We began to play.

"Where'd you learn all these card games?" I asked, surveying my hand.

"I taught myself. I have several books on playing cards," she said, and laid down a king of clubs. "They're an Earth pastime that I rather enjoy." I glanced up at her.

"Are you not from Earth?" I asked. Flatwoods's chest buzzed. I got the impression it was her version of a chuckle. I almost said something about how I grew up in the Creek so I don't go around assuming everyone who isn't human is from outer space, but she spoke before I could get the words out.

"No, if you couldn't tell, I'm not from Earth," she answered, her tone dry. Her voice sounded a little more staticky than usual, like whatever radio station she was tuned to was just barely in range. She sounded—sad wasn't quite the word. Maybe something more like melancholy; thoughtful. Like she was half lost in a memory.

"Where are you from?" I asked. I placed a card on top of hers.

"Very far away," she said. She didn't sound angry, but there was a finality to her statement, as if there just wasn't anything more to say. I'd never been more than a few hours from home. I went to school here, had all my friends and family here, worked here. In my whole life, I'd never really had the occasion to feel homesick, to be far from the place and people I loved.

I glanced at Flatwoods again. This time I noticed the small dents in her headdress, the flecks of rust on her shoulders, the spot at the edge of her left eye that no longer lit up. I saw the way the house, already cavernous and dark, seemed to bend around her, to grow larger. As I sat, I began to hear the clanging sound again. Very faint at first, but it grew louder as Flatwoods placed her next card. The sound was definitely coming from her.

"Flatwoods," I said softly. She looked up at me but the clanging continued. "That's the sound I heard earlier," I said. She went quiet.

"Ah," she said. She placed a hand on her forehead in an embarrassed way. "I didn't realize I was doing it."

"What does that noise mean?" I asked. I hoped the question didn't sound rude. She rubbed her hand over her forehead and I flinched at the sound of metal on metal.

"I was—what would you call it." She thought for a moment. "I was humming."

I had to admit, there was a part of me that wanted to dislike Flatwoods. A sticky little piece of my heart that knew it would be simpler if I could just think of her as the villain, offer her no sympathy, see in her no growth. But the image of Flatwoods, alone at her kitchen table, playing solitaire and humming to herself, lodged itself in my chest.

We played for a few more minutes in silence, until I said I had to get back to work. Flatwoods just nodded and reshuffled the cards. She was starting a new solitaire game before I had even left the kitchen.

Just outside my room, I heard a noise behind me. I turned to see a dark figure a few yards down the hall. From its height I assumed it was Flatwoods. I was about to call out, but when I blinked the figure vanished.

It had officially been a week. A full week of failure after failure, séance after tarot reading after tea leaf reading after food offering after desperate Ouija board session where I just set the board on my bed and cried. I decided I'd give it one more night and if I couldn't find anything, I'd give Flatwoods back her money and retire in shame.

For my last night, I decided to strip down my approach. I would only bring a candle. I would set up in front of the grand staircase, a place that felt very liminal. I told Flatwoods my plan, and to my surprise she asked to join me.

It was just after dusk and the house was dark. A storm had moved in during the afternoon. Rain sluiced down the windows and thunder rumbled ominously. Flatwoods and I sat on the chipped parquet floor, just out of arm's reach of each other. Between us, I lit a single candle.

"Spirit, if you're out there, please reveal yourself," I said to the darkness around us. "Please. I'm begging you." The house was silent. Outside, the storm picked up and the thunder got louder. Every few minutes I would make a plea to the spirit. Every few minutes I was ignored. Soon, the thunder was loud enough to shake the house. Above us, a cobwebbed chandelier swayed slightly. The occasional bolt of lightning turned Flatwoods eerily pale. In her smooth, metal face I thought I could see something worse than her earlier disapproval: her pity.

"I'm sorry," I said finally. "I don't think I can do it." I put my face in my hands. I'd never failed like this before, failed so completely and miserably at the one thing I was supposed to be good at. I really didn't want to cry in front of Flatwoods, but I could feel tears pricking the corners of my eyes.

"I'm supposed to be an *expert*," I said, "I'm supposed to be able to help you no matter what." Flatwoods scoffed and I finally looked up. "Could you not laugh in my face right now?" I snapped.

"I just—I think it's silly to put that much pressure on yourself," she said. I stared at her. "Nobody's flawlessly good at anything. You're doing your best." She turned her head slightly so she wasn't looking directly at me.

The rain slammed against the windows. I tried to focus on Flatwoods, on what she'd just said, on the slight dimming of her eyes and the angle of her head. Something about the way she held herself—if she could blush, I knew she'd be blushing. In that moment, everything finally clicked together in my brain. Flatwoods wasn't needling me about everything because she was a dick. She was teasing me. She was flirting. Not very well, but flirting. She just happened to pick on everything I couldn't handle being picked on for. Every time I'd been the most annoyed with her, it was because of my own baggage. And maybe she was also a dick. Both things could be true.

As I was having this realization, thunder erupted overhead, louder than I'd ever heard it. A searingly bright light came in through the window. We were plunged back into darkness. The last thing I saw before the lights went out was Flatwoods.

For a moment, neither of us moved. My heart was racing and my ears were ringing. Or—it wasn't my ears that were ringing. It was my phone, where I'd left it plugged into the wall in the sitting room. I scrambled into the room and picked up my phone. The screen was bright green and the text looked smudged and weird. Before I could think about it much more, I swiped my thumb to answer the phone call.

A loud voice, much louder than any sound my phone could make, filled the room.

"Hello?" it called. "Hello, are you there?" There was a pause, and then another sound—even louder than the voice—a discordant clanging.

"Mom?" said Flatwoods's voice from behind me. I turned to stare at her with wide eyes. She glided over and took the phone from me.

"My dear! Finally! We finally got ahold of you!" she shouted. I winced at the volume. "Your mother and I have been trying to reach you for months. We can't figure out how your Earth phones work," she said. Flatwoods sighed.

"Mom, I explained this to you before. You have to—"

"We tried astral projecting already, but I think you're out of range. We couldn't manage to do anything besides slam doors and knock things over. Why did you have to move somewhere so far away?" Flatwoods sighed again as her mom carried on.

Suddenly I was struck with a bolt of clarity. This wasn't *Sixth Sense*, it was *Close Encounters of the Third Kind*. I could see on Flatwoods's face that she was coming to the same conclusion. I could also see that she was pointedly trying to avoid looking at me.

"It's good to hear from you, Mom," she interrupted. "I thought you weren't calling because you were avoiding me or something."

"Avoiding you!" a higher-pitched voice exclaimed from the other end of the line. "Why would we be avoiding you!"

"Hi, Mom Two," Flatwoods said. She turned away sheepishly. I took the hint to give her some space and retreated to my room.

The next morning, I found Flatwoods in the kitchen, replacing the lightbulbs. She didn't look up when I came in.

"So," I said, "I guess we figured out what's haunting this place. Is it a good thing or a bad thing that it's just your parents?"

Flatwoods sighed and a deep buzzing sound came from her chest. "I've been giving you a hard time and all along it was my problem."

"Yeah, it's kinda like this whole time you were needling me to call my mom, when actually you needed to call your mom," I said. For an alarming second, Flatwoods was silent. I mentally prepared for her to banish me from her house. Then, finally, she laughed. I realized it was a sound I hadn't heard before, a short beeping like the sound of dialing a phone number on a landline. I laughed too, happy to hear this new sound from her.

"I guess this means you're leaving?" she asked when she had finished giggling.

"I don't live too far away," I said, suddenly unable to meet her eyes. "I'm right down the hill if you ever want to, I don't know, hang out sometime." Now that I'd finished my job, I felt good. I felt like there were a lot more possibilities in the world than I'd originally thought. Space aliens could call my cell phone, so. Probably anything could happen. Even me and Flatwoods.

I looked up when I heard her whir closer to me.

"I'd like that," she said. She was standing close to me, and she was so tall. And so shiny. I loved the way her metal exterior glowed faintly under the kitchen lights. I loved the sounds she made, even the clanging, especially her funny beeping laugh. It turns out I was really, really into her. "I'd really like to keep seeing you."

I pulled myself onto the counter at my back so I could be closer to her height. Then I reached up and kissed her. And kissed her. And it was electric.

YEARN FOR IT

I've recently taken up smoking just to have an excuse to stand in the alley behind Bone Broth with the hot line cook. I don't love the taste of the cigarettes, but I love watching smoke trail out of his mouth. Today, the spring sunshine makes him look particularly stunning, and even though I know I'm being obvious about it, I can't stop staring.

Cactus Cat is basically my dream guy. His shoulders are slumped under his T-shirts, his jeans hang a little low around his hips, his eyes always have dark circles around them. His skin is made of overlapping peyote cacti—I know this because I looked it up—and the dumpling-shaped plants give him a certain softness that makes him seem approachable, even though his sleepy eyes have a glint of menace. (Hot menace.) He has two smaller peyotes growing from the top of his head like little ears, and several that protrude from the base of his spine like a tail. He's soft, not prickly—the only cactus spines on his body are his claws.

He's the loveliest shade of green and his voice is soft with a slight rasp. I could go on. The point is that he's perfect.

"Would that work?" he asks, and I realize he'd been talking to me. I was too focused on watching his jaw move to hear what he was saying. I take a long drag on my cigarette to seem relaxed.

"What's up?" I ask as I exhale. He grins like he knows why I wasn't listening. His teeth are sharp and white.

"I said my friend is having a house party tonight and you should come," he repeats. He leans a shoulder against the brick wall of the restaurant, his posture relaxed, easy. He must know how hot he looks like this.

Under normal circumstances, I would've been all over him. But last week I made a bet with my best friend, Mason. We've both been slutting it up a lot, and it's been fun but also exhausting. To get us back on our feet, Mason suggested that we see who can go the longest without hooking up with anyone. The bet is for fifty dollars, and while I'd rather keep my fifty dollars, my real motivation is the fact that I hate losing. Especially to Mason.

Mason is the only person I know who might be cooler than me. He's the kind of guy who's always at least six months ahead of the trend. I've always prided myself on my good taste, but I'm basically a normie compared to him. Plus, he's super hot and his body count is crazy. If he wasn't my best friend he would be my archenemy. I wouldn't be his archenemy, because he's too sweet to have enemies, but he'd be mine. I don't plan to lose this bet.

"I don't know," I say hesitantly.

"Come on, Romy," CC says. He reaches out and touches my elbow. He does it so casually, like he's touched me a thousand times before. Only he hasn't. This is the first time we've ever touched. His skin is cool and smooth. His claws brush my arm as he removes his hand. They feel like little briars—right on the line between ticklish and stinging. Goosebumps erupt down my arm.

"Okay," I say quickly, almost automatically. I feel myself blush. He smiles and brings his cigarette to his lips. I do the same. We exhale and our smoke tangles together in the cool air. He's looking at me thoughtfully, like he's trying to figure something out. I hold his gaze. His eyes are green as his skin. In the afternoon sun, they flash in a way that feels dangerous. Fifty dollars' worth of dangerous.

"I can pick you up at nine if that works?" he offers. I accept. We put out our cigarettes and go back to work.

Inside, the lunch rush has just hit. I love working at Bone Broth, even when it's busy like this. Actually, I especially love it when it's busy like this. I like having to think on my feet and parse my own shitty handwriting on my order pad and remember the names of all our regulars. My brain works best when it's moving at a hundred miles an hour. Plus, in a ramen shop, there's always the smell of noodles and pork broth floating in the air, a warm, comforting scent that makes me hungry no matter how long my shift is. When I get home I always smell like freshly sliced green onions, ginger, toasted sesame oil, and the light, sweet scent of menma.

Just after the lunch rush and just before CC's shift is over, Mason wanders into the restaurant. He's wearing an outfit that would look stupid on anyone else but on him it looks both cool and effortless. It's a very large T-shirt that he screen printed the words *big boy* onto, along with a pair of indecently short shorts, a pink bandana tied around his neck like an ascot, and a very lumpy cardigan that he clearly made himself. If I saw someone else wearing this, I would go out of my way not to talk to them. But Mason somehow avoids looking like the most annoying guy in the room.

"Hi, Romy," he says, grabbing a seat at the counter. He gives me a big smile and pushes his hair out of his eyes. "Lose any bets lately?" I roll my eyes and fill his water glass.

"I'm not planning on losing any bets, ever," I say. "Plus, I'm working all the time. How am I gonna meet somebody when I'm always at work?" It's at this exact moment that CC comes out of the kitchen. He has on an old windbreaker and a baseball cap with holes cut out for his ears. His hands are buried in his pockets.

"I'll pick you up at nine, yeah?" he asks as he walks by. I can feel Mason's eyes burning into me, but I keep my gaze on CC. He's walking backwards toward the door, waiting for my response.

"Yeah, nine sounds good," I say. He nods and pushes the door open with his elbow. He has this lazy, languid way of moving that makes everything he does seem like an afterthought. I'm still watching him when the door closes and Mason leans across the counter to me.

"How am I gonna meet somebody when I'm always at work?" he mimics. I roll my eyes again, but it's less convincing this time.

"He's just a friend," I mumble. Mason laughs.

"Sure. Do you look at all your friends like that?" he asks.

"Like what?" I ask. Mason laughs again.

"Whatever you say, dude. I know you yearn for him," he says. I throw a menu at him.

"Are you going to order something or did you just come here to harass me?" Now it's his turn to roll his eyes.

"I'll order. But my next few lunches are gonna be on you when you lose this bet," he says. I take his order quickly and stomp back to the kitchen. I can be friends with hot people. Mason's hot, and we're just friends. Well, mostly we're just friends. Like eighty-twenty. But me and CC will be just friends all the time, nothing fishy going on. This will be a very chill, very chaste friendship. I can do it. I drink a glass of cold water and leave the kitchen.

I put a lot of effort into making my outfit seem low effort that night. I settle on a black crop top and a tight black skirt that makes my ass look actually perfect. I throw a big denim shirt over everything because maybe the skirt makes my ass look a little too perfect. How perfect should one's ass look when one is hanging out with a platonic friend?

CC knocks on my door at 9:05. I think it's hot that he was punctual, and then I try to forget I thought it was hot that he was punctual. I open the door and he's wearing a cropped bowling shirt and flared corduroys. The outfit surprises me. I'm used to seeing him in T-shirts and jeans and his apron. I just assumed he dresses simply even on his off-hours, but this is a legitimate outfit.

"Cool pants," I say.

"Cool skirt," he replies. I step outside and lock the door behind me. We walk together in silence for a while. When we do talk, our conversations are stilted and a little awkward, the way conversations tend to be on a first date. Except, of course, this isn't a date. It's just two well-dressed friends going to a party. I focus very hard on not walking too close to him.

After what feels like a very long walk, we finally arrive at CC's friend's house. Inside, the party's already started. It seems like half the town is crammed into this little bungalow. Music plays loudly and the bass thumps in my chest. It's a song Mason recommended to me around this time last year. The house is hot and full of plants. It's lit mostly by colored fairy lights that look like they were hung up moments before the party started. It's a cool vibe, very classic house party. Like something out of a movie.

"There should be drinks in the kitchen," CC says, his mouth suddenly right against my ear. His breath is hot on my cheek, his body nearly but not quite touching mine. I manage to nod. He takes my hand and leads us to the kitchen. When he touches me, I feel like I'm floating in a beam of light, like there's a disco ball sparkling in my chest. I look at our hands clasped together, his lush green skin and the spines that grow from the tips of his fingers like nails. My brown skin and black nails and unruly pile of little gold bracelets. Our hands look good together.

CC pulls me through the crowd and into a small kitchen at the back of the house. The sink is filled with ice and piled with beer and seltzer. We both take lime seltzers and smile shyly at each other when we realize we picked the same thing.

"Lime is my favorite flavor," I say, leaning close to his face so he can hear me. He has to hunch a bit so my mouth is closer to his ear. He grins at me.

"I know," he says into my ear, "you always get those lime sodas when you eat at work." I look at him, processing the fact that he noticed such a small detail about me. If my face wasn't already hot from the party, I know I would be blushing. He's looking at me—*into* me, really. His pupils are vertical, like a cat's. In the dim light they're wider than usual. One of his hands rests on the counter behind me. I move a little closer to him, still looking into his eyes. He has an intent look on his face, his normally relaxed features rearranged in intense focus. He's never looked at me like this before and it's doing something to me. His thumb brushes the small of my back.

"CC!" a voice calls. The spell is broken. CC blinks and looks away. I take a split second to study the line of his jaw and then follow his gaze to where the Jersey Devil is standing. He waves and she pushes her way through the kitchen to us. This must be his friend who's hosting the party. I've seen her a few times at the plant store. Tonight, she has some kind of cute, shimmery powder sprinkled on her bat-like wings and her curling goat's horns.

The Jersey Devil hugs him and they chat for a bit until CC

gestures to me and says, "This is Romy. We work together." This is a correct description of our relationship, but I was secretly bummed that he hadn't introduced me as *Romy, the hottest waitress I've ever worked with*, or *Romy, the girl I'm secretly in love with except it's not a secret anymore because I've finally found the courage to say it out loud—Romy, I love you. Will you travel the world with me so we can make out and eat delicious food and be together forever and never die?* Something like that.

I snap out of my fantasy to find the Jersey Devil offering me her hand and telling me to call her Jersey. I tell her it's nice to meet her. She glances at CC, then to me, then back to CC again.

"If you two want to go somewhere a little quieter, I don't think there's too many people in the backyard," she says, pointing to a door to our left. She smiles in a way that could have been innocent, except for the glint in her eye. I desperately want to go somewhere a little quieter with CC. But then I imagine Mason in his *big boy* T-shirt, listening to whatever band is going to be huge next year, laughing at me while he takes my money. I take a big sip of my seltzer.

"I want to dance," CC says. Jersey's brow furrows, but she keeps her polite smile.

"Don't let me stop you," she says. Someone at the other end of the room calls her name and she leaves us.

"Do you really want to dance?" I ask.

"I love dancing," he says. "You're not one of those people who refuses to dance, are you?"

"I'm not very good," I say nervously. It's hard to be a cool guy who also dances at parties. Mason does it, but he doesn't have to put any effort into being the cool guy.

"It'll be fun. If you hate it, we'll stop," he says. He takes my hand again. His cactus skin is cool to the touch. In the heat of the party, his hand is a relief. I don't want to let it go. I let him lead me back into the living room.

It actually is fun dancing with CC. For a while we're mostly focused on making each other laugh. Every time I do something silly, he giggles and I forget to feel embarrassed. The space is crowded but all my attention is on him. We drink and dance and laugh. Without my noticing it, we move closer. I have my arms around his neck and he has his arms around my waist and we're swaying. I have no idea if we're moving in time to the music or not. I'm oblivious to everything in the room except for CC, his green eyes, his scratchy laugh, and the feeling of his soft hands on my waist.

A sheen of sweat covers his face and chest and I know that if I put my lips on his skin he'll taste sweet like agave. I lick my lips. He looks at me with his pupils blown wide, his eyes following the movement of my tongue. He's rubbing circles on the small of my back with his thumb. I shiver. Our faces are getting closer and closer, and when he smiles, I can see his sharp white teeth, and I want to put my tongue in his mouth and run it over his fangs. I gently run my nails over the back of his neck and he closes his eyes in pleasure. I dig my nails in a little harder and he sighs audibly and leans his head on my shoulder. His hands move just a little lower, resting on the place where my waist becomes my ass. His breath is hot on my neck. There's no space left between us; we're completely intertwined. There's nothing left inside me. I've been hollowed out by want.

I'm thinking about how I've probably never been more into anyone in my life when someone bumps into me and spills a warm beer down my back.

I gasp, equally surprised by the beer and the reminder that there are other people in the room. I turn to see a yeti with a shocked and apologetic look on his face. He apologizes and tries to help clean me up, but I tell him it's fine, I need to leave anyway. Because I do need to leave. I need to get away from CC immediately, before I take this any further.

"I should head out," I say to CC. He nods. He blinks like he's coming out of a trance.

"Do you want me to walk you home?" he asks.

"No, it's fine. Stay here and hang out. It's not that late," I say. He offers again, just to be sure, but I turn him down again. The last thing I need is to be totally alone with him. I hope the walk home alone in the cool air clears my head.

At work, the vibe is undeniably flirty. His hand brushes my waist when he moves past me, his fingers linger on mine when he hands me a bowl of ramen. I catch him staring at me more than once. Sometimes it's the fact that he isn't touching me, that he's so close but keeping himself perfectly out of reach. Like he knows exactly where his body ends and mine begins. Sometimes flirting is a contact sport, but with CC it's a dance. Near and then far and then near again. I'm constantly on edge, constantly flushed, constantly aware of his eyes on me.

He's got me doing crazy shit. I've winked at him repeatedly just because it makes him blush darker green. One day at lunch he challenged me to see who could drink their broth faster and I just did it without hesitation, and afterwards I got broth in my nose from laughing. Sometimes he puts little sticky notes on my locker with dumb drawings on them, so I started putting little origami cranes at his work station. It is deeply elementary school, deeply uncool stuff. Stuff I never would've thought he would be into. But the thing about CC is that he's always totally himself. I think that's why he's so chill all the time. I would be super relaxed too if I was that comfortable with myself.

One night about two weeks into our flirtationship, we're the only two on the closing shift. The weather's been bad so business is slow, and by the late evening we're the only two in the restaurant. I'm sitting at the counter, folding old receipts into origami cranes. He's puttering around in the back. I jump when he sets a bowl of ramen next to me.

"I put extra menma in yours. That's how you like it, right?" he asks. I nod. He puts two lime sodas down, one in front of each of us. A trail of warmth moves through my chest. Usually when I flirt with someone, I'm mostly focused on the eventual hookup. I like flirting, but it's a means to an end. CC treats flirting like it's an end all to itself. He works at it, commits to it. He's genuinely interested in me. And even though I would love to be hot and heavy, I have to admit I'm enjoying the slow burn. It makes every little touch so much sweeter. I take a sip of the soup.

We eat quietly until we finish our noodles. CC brings his bowl to his mouth and drinks the broth. He tips his head back and reveals the curved lines of cactus that make up his neck. My skin goes hot. He puts down his bowl and wipes his chin with the back of his wrist.

"I also grabbed this," he says, and places a bottle of sake and two small cups in front of us. "I don't think the manager will care if we have a drink or two." I grin.

"I didn't realize you were such a troublemaker," I say.

"Don't get too excited. I grabbed the cheapest stuff," he says, and pours us both a cup. He angles himself so he's facing me, so his knee is between my legs. We cheers and throw the shots back. Warmth blooms in my stomach and my body immediately feels looser. CC rolls his neck. I try not to imagine running a finger along his jawline. I try not to feel his thumb lightly tapping my wrist. I try not to think about the fact that his body is only a few inches away. I try not to lose myself when he looks into my eyes and blinks very slowly. I realized we're both leaning in.

"Wait," I blurt. He pauses and looks at me curiously, his pupils two little slits. "I can't kiss you—I mean, I can't actually touch you at all—well, not like I *can't* touch you, just—" I stop when he leans away from me. More than leans away. He retreats from me, withdrawing his knee from between my legs, crossing his arms, sitting straighter on his stool. His brows are knit together in concern.

"We don't have to do anything you don't want to do," he says. He says it so earnestly and sweetly that I immediately feel calmer.

"It's not that," I say, trying to think of how to explain this ridiculous situation. "I made this stupid bet with a friend. If I hook up with someone before he does, I lose. It's dumb, but I just—Mason's going to be so annoying if he wins," I say. He's quiet for a moment, processing. His eyes search mine.

"Does this mean you're into me?" he asks finally. I feel my face erupt in a blush when I nod. I look away, embarrassed.

"Romy," he says, but I don't look at him. He gently touches my chin and turns my head to face him. The sake swimming around in my chest does a flip. "Romy, I'm so into you," he says when I finally manage to look him in the eyes.

"We can't touch," I say quickly. He pulls his finger away, the claw scraping gently against my chin.

"We can't touch at all? I thought the bet was about hooking up," he says.

"It is about hooking up. It's just that . . ." I lean back and sigh. "It's just that if I touch you, I'm going to want to do more than just touch you." My face burns. My gaze flicks to his and I see a mix of surprise and something else in his face. Something darker and more tender. A blaze of heat runs through me.

"What else would you want to do to me?" he asks, the look in his eyes growing darker still. My breath catches in my chest. The room tilts on its axis. Desire moves through me like a living thing, unspooling in my chest and slithering below my stomach. It's hot and viscous and sweet. It leaves a trail of wet.

He shifts his body closer to me. "I can tell you what I want to do to you," he says, his voice a raspy whisper. He gently bumps his knee against my inner thigh, as if to remind me it's there. I've never been so turned on in my life. It's like he knows exactly what to say, exactly where to look at me to make me melt. His eyes trace the line of my throat when I swallow nervously. He watches my lips when I speak. It's a level of intimacy that I haven't felt before, and it's almost overwhelming.

"Romy, I want to give you whatever you want. But I won't give it to you unless you ask for it," he says. I think for a moment, biting my lip, watching him watch me bite my lip. His hand is at my elbow, his claws drawing little circles on my skin. I shiver.

"I don't want to lose," I whisper. He raises an eyebrow but gives me a small smile.

"Then I don't want you to lose," he says simply. He stands and walks back to the kitchen without another word. I briefly leave my body. My brain is trying to process what just happened. I picture CC's soft green lips, his rough cat's tongue.

Why did I just say that? Because of a stupid bet? I'm willing to sacrifice fifty dollars. At this moment, I'd give up basically anything to have CC. The realization comes over me in a wave: I want to lose this bet. I want very, very badly to lose. In fact, I'm even looking forward to losing this bet. So what if I have to admit defeat to Mason? He won't care, he'll be more interested in hearing about CC. I come crashing back into my body. I laugh at myself for being so dumb.

When I throw open the door to the kitchen, CC looks up.

"I want you to kiss me," I tell him. He's across the room in two quick strides. He holds my face in his hands and my cheeks cool a little at his touch.

"Is that all you want?" he asks, his voice teasing. I laugh. Our faces are so close, nearly touching. I can smell the green, sweet scent of his skin and the tang of sake on his breath. I feel dazed but also completely focused, like I'm walking through fog following a single trail of light. He leans in closer.

"I want—" I start, and the bell over the front door jingles. We both freeze. I completely forgot the restaurant was still open. I can see in CC's face that he's thinking the same thing. The customer clears their throat, waiting in the dining room. Slowly, CC and I separate. We both drop our hands to our sides, and CC straightens his apron.

"I should go," I say. He nods. I'm about to open the kitchen door when CC stops me.

"Wait—give me your hand," he says. I hold out my right hand and he gently takes it and turns it over so my palm is up. He leans his face toward my wrist. When he's a fraction of an inch from making contact, he pauses. His eyes flick up to mine.

"Is this okay?" he asks. Seeing him like this, his lips nearly on my skin, his eyes big and focused on me, his pupils blown wide, I can barely control myself. I nod. He kisses my wrist, gently but certainly, his lips warm against my skin. I inhale sharply. Desire slithers through me once again.

With what seemed to be a not insignificant amount of effort, he raises his head back up and releases my hand.

"Sorry," he says, his voice gravelly and caught in his throat. "I just really wanted to touch you." I nod, incapable of forming words. Before either of us can do anything else, I hurry into the dining room. We finish our shift in silence, never touching, our bodies still reacting to each other even with all the space between them.

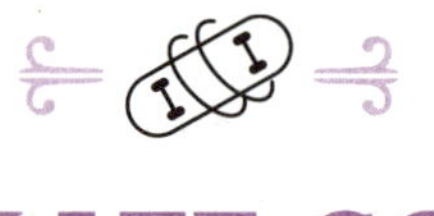

SKATE GOD

My mom doesn't like it when I kick the front door open, but today I do it anyway. I'm too excited to do anything slowly. Tonight will be my first time at the skate park. Tonight I become a skater.

Today was my fifteenth birthday, and my mom got me a used skateboard. I've tried being a lot of different things. I was goth, but I got tired of the eyeliner. I played soccer, but my teammates said I played too rough. We don't talk about my very short time as a weeb. But I'm confident that skateboarding will be the thing for me. It's cool, physical, vaguely social but not team-oriented, and it has its own aesthetic. Plus I might get some cool scars doing it.

I spent a lot of time thinking about what to wear tonight. My brother said I'm not allowed in his room while he's at college, but I figured he wouldn't notice if I borrowed just one shirt. Skater clothes are supposed to be oversized—I know because

Fresno

I've been staking out the skate park. Not in, like, a creepy way. I just want to know what's up.

I find an old blue and purple striped rugby shirt in his closet that comes down to my knees. It's perfect. I tuck it into my baggiest pair of jeans and coax my hair into two little puffs at the nape of my neck. Looking at myself in the mirror, I see a real skater. The genuine article. Someone who was born to do this.

My mom yells at me when I kick open the door with my old checkered Vans, but I just keep going. The streetlamps click on right as I step outside. It's spring and the air is cool but not cold. From half a block away, I can already tell that the skate park is busy. I hear the sharp noise of wheels grinding on cement, wood scraping across metal, shouting and laughter. I slow down.

For a second, I feel nervous. Contrary to what other people seem to think, I get scared a lot. I'm never afraid of a *physical* challenge. What I'm *very* afraid of is other people. Other people feel like they exist in some kind of parallel dimension, like I can see them but only through a thick, shimmery cloud. I don't know how to make it so we're both in the same dimension. I can jump off the roof of the supply shed or skitch on my old roller skates or climb the tallest tree in town no problem. What I can't seem to do is make anyone like me.

A cheer rises up from the skate park. I take a deep breath. Before I can have another thought, I start walking. It's always best to do these things without thinking. Thinking only makes things worse.

I slip through the gate of the chain-link fence surrounding

the park and look around. I recognize a few people from around town, like the lady that owns the karaoke bar. By the far edge of the park is a group of kids and nightcrawlers I recognize from school. I've always thought nightcrawlers look like sheet ghosts wearing pants, since they're just blobby heads attached to two legs and they have big, dark eyes that kind of look like they were drawn on with a marker. Tonight, I notice they glow white under the yellow sodium lamps.

Nightcrawlers are notoriously good at skateboarding. In the couple of minutes that I'm watching them, I see one of them ride a rail for longer than I've ever seen anyone ride a rail. I pick a spot far away from them. I would look doubly stupid if I screwed up in front of the skateboarding geniuses.

I put on my helmet because I promised my mom I'd wear it. I set one foot on the board and roll it back and forth a few times to get a feel for it. Carefully, I step my other foot onto the board. I wiggle a little to make myself move back and forth. This isn't so hard. I can definitely do this. I take my right foot off the board and push. I'm skating! Okay, I'm skating very slowly in a straight line, but still. I try to suppress a smile and push again.

Just as I'm thinking what a natural I am at this, my board shoots out from under me. I'm suddenly lying on my back on the concrete. I gasp for breath. The stars wobble overhead.

"You good?" someone asks. I sit up. A nightcrawler is standing in front of me, my board at his feet. He's wearing cuffed chinos and a cool T-shirt with flames on it. The shirt's sleeves hang limp because he doesn't have any arms. His voice is warm and a little rough. This isn't just any boy: this is *Fresno,* one of the most popular guys in my grade. I hadn't seen him earlier, but now he's taking up my entire field of vision.

"Good," I reply as my face flushes. Fresno gently kicks my skateboard to me.

"First time skating?" he asks. My face gets hotter but I nod. "That's cool. I like when people want to learn how to skate." I glance up at him to see if he's joking, but his big eyes look serious.

"I just got this skateboard today. For my birthday," I add, then feel silly for saying it. Fresno grins.

"Happy birthday," he says. "Would you wanna, like, hang with me and my friends over there?" He nods his head toward his group. My brain fizzles out for a second.

I don't even remember the last time somebody asked me to hang out. Nobody's ever mean to me, but nobody ever wants to hang out with me either. I haven't had a birthday party since the nightmare year when I turned thirteen and invited my whole class to go swimming at the lake. Nobody came. The whole day was just me and my mom and my brother sitting alone by the water. I ate a whole sheet cake by myself and threw up in the bushes. Then we went home.

I realize I've been quiet for a little too long, so I nod and stand up. I've never been this close to Fresno before. He only comes up to my chin. This close, I can see that his skin is a little gooey, like he's covered in a thick layer of gel.

"I'm Fresno, by the way," he says. I try to act like someone learning this information for the first time.

"I'm Sloane," I respond.

"Cool name," says Fresno. "Sloane, this is Ollie and Jude"—he nods at nightcrawlers—"and this is AJ"—he nods at a human.

"I think we have math class together," Jude said.

"Yeah, and we all have English together," said AJ, gesturing to themself, me, and Ollie. I nod. I'm nervous to say anything in case I say the wrong thing.

"Sloane's just learning to skate," Fresno says. "I figured she could hang with us and we could show her some stuff." The group nods.

"Show us what you can do so far," says Jude. He's a little taller than Fresno and wears a tattered bucket hat and oversized cargo shorts.

I stand with both feet on my board. "That's basically it," I say.

"Can you push?" asks Jude.

"That's how I fell down," I say. Fresno laughs. He has a nice laugh. It's kind of raspy, and it echoes around the park a little bit louder than it should.

"Skating is mostly falling down," he says. "But it's chill, I'll teach you what you need to know." My heart flutters.

"Cool" is all I manage to say.

For the next few hours, I hang out with Fresno and Jude and Ollie and AJ and they teach me how to skate. Ollie knows a lot about the mechanics of the board itself, and keeps asking me questions about my wheels and recommending different trucks and grip tape. AJ is apparently really good at all kinds of skating. They also roller skate and scooter—they kept reiterating that they "love going fast." Jude is just a straight-up incredible skater. He moves so gracefully that he looks weightless. I've never seen anybody skate like him but it's almost hypnotic to watch.

I learn the most from Fresno. He's good at talking me through things, and he sticks with me when the others get distracted by their own stuff. He stands close to me, directing me by pointing with his sneakers or demonstrating on his own board. I ask him if it's hard to skate without arms to help you balance or catch you when you fall. He thinks about this for a second.

"This is the only way I know how to do it," he says. "I never really thought about whether it was harder. I just knew I liked skating, so I skated." I watch his mouth half form his words as he speaks. When nightcrawlers talk, their mouths don't move quite right around their words. It's like maybe their voices are coming from somewhere else in their bodies. "What made you want to start skating?" he asks. I flush.

"I thought it seemed cool," I say lamely. But Fresno nods thoughtfully like I said something actually meaningful.

"Yeah, it is cool. There's a lot of cool people who hang out here. It's chill that you wanted to hang out here too," he says. I glance at him, but he's looking at his high-tops.

I really like how relaxed Fresno is. I'm not relaxed and sometimes it freaks me out to be around people who are too laid-back. I feel like they're judging me. But I don't feel like Fresno is judging me one way or the other. There's no pressure to be any particular type of way.

"Can you teach me a trick?" I ask. He laughs at this, and I

privately thrill to hear his laugh again.

"Yeah, I'll teach you a trick. It's called 'stay standing on your board while it's in motion.'" He shoots me a sly grin.

"Okay, I've heard that's actually really hard," I say dramatically. He laughs again.

"I believe in you," he says, and taps my board with his toe. By the end of the night, I've gotten pretty good at this trick.

Over the next few weeks, I spend more and more time at the skate park. I hang out with Fresno and his friends and get (slowly, painfully, incrementally) better at skating. Everyone takes turns showing me the basics and they never seem to get annoyed with how long it takes me to learn every little thing. They're all patient and encouraging, even when they're teasing me. I still haven't managed to drop into the bowl yet, but I can skate on flat ground mostly without falling, and I'm okay at turning.

It's crazy to have friends. I can't believe I have a group of friends that I get to see every day, friends who are always glad to see me and think I'm funny even when I do stupid stuff. I love gossiping with AJ and watching them do kickflips. I love that Jude has started sitting next to me in math class. I love that Ollie asked me to cut the sleeves off his T-shirts since "muscle tees are cool right now" and he "doesn't have arms anyway."

And, of course, there's Fresno. When I'm around him, I feel like it doesn't matter what weird thing I say or how mid I am at skating. He seems happy to just be hanging. He's comfortable;

comforting. I've never felt like this before. Like the shimmering cloud is a little less solid, like I can almost reach into that other dimension. I'm afraid it's only a matter of time before I do something to wreck it.

One day I'm talking to Ollie and AJ while we watch Fresno and Jude skate.

"Okay, I'm not trying to be, like, gossipy," AJ whispers, and I laugh. Whenever AJ starts a sentence like this, it means they're about to say something incredibly petty. "I'm not!" they protest. "But I've just been wondering, like, what's up with you and Fresno?" AJ and Ollie are both looking at me.

"What do you mean what's up with me and Fresno? Did he say something?" I feel a pit forming in my stomach. Is Fresno mad at me about something? AJ and Ollie exchange a glance.

"Obviously I'm not trying to be heteronormative and say that since you're hanging out with a boy you *must* have a crush on him," says AJ.

"Obviously not," says Ollie.

"It's just that it kinda seems like Fresno's into you? I mean, he's not easy to read, but I think he might be into you. He hangs out with you, like, a lot," AJ says. Ollie says something in agreement, but I can't hear what it is. My ears are ringing. Time is going really slow and really fast all at once. I feel more feelings at one time than I've ever felt before. It's like my insides are loose and sloshing around. Like I'm being filled up with wet cement, but in a good way. Maybe in a good way? I've lost track of how I'm supposed to feel.

My last hobby before skateboarding was soccer. I used to hang out with this one boy on my team a lot. He was really intense, like how I was, so we got along. We were always daring each other to do stuff, like really stupid stuff, like drink a whole water bottle in one gulp or eat dirt or do a flip. Just whatever we thought was funny. We would get in trouble with our coach for bodychecking on the field. But it was fun. I liked having someone who wanted to hang out with me, even if it was mostly just during practice.

But then I heard some of my teammates talking about how they thought I was in love with him. It wasn't that I was grossed out by the idea of being with this guy—although I really wasn't into him—it was more that I didn't like them talking about me, speculating about my life and my feelings. It was embarrassing in a way I still can't really put into words. It made me feel like everyone was looking at me, everyone in the world, and they were all trying to pry open my head and see my brain. It was like there was some megahivemind that everyone else was tapped into except for me, and they were all focusing their hivemind on judging me.

During practice that day I bodychecked the guy extra hard, so that nobody would think I liked him. Unfortunately, I pushed him so hard that he hit the ground and knocked a tooth out. There was a lot of blood and a lot of people yelling at me. I wasn't allowed back at practice. The guy never talked to me again. In one fell swoop I lost my hobby and the closest thing I'd ever had to a friend. I gave up on my dream of being a cool jock. I moved on to the next dream.

There's a scraping sound and, suddenly, Fresno pops out of the bowl and lands in front of me. He looks up from under his stupid little corduroy baseball hat with his big stupid eyes. And he's smiling. At me. I grimace back.

"Hey, it's you," he says.

"It's you, too," I say, and he smiles bigger. My stomach twists.

"Do you want me to show you how to do a kickflip?" Fresno asks. I glance over at AJ and see them exchange a look with Ollie. My whole body tenses. A wave of fear rises up inside me and blocks out all the light. I can't think straight.

"Why would I need you to show me how to do a kickflip?" I snap before I can stop myself. Fresno looks confused.

"We were talking about it last week, so I thought—" he starts. I cut him off.

"I don't remember every conversation I have with you," I say. I can't meet his eyes.

"Oh. My bad," he says uncertainly. I've never talked to him like this. I can tell he's trying to meet my gaze and figure out what is wrong, but I don't move my eyes from his forehead.

"It's not like you're some kind of skate god," I say, my vision going a little wobbly around the edges. "I don't need you to teach me how to do everything." Everyone goes quiet. Fresno nods slowly, clearly thinking something over.

"Yeah. My bad, I guess," he says. He kicks off and rolls away. Nobody talks for another few seconds.

Then: "What was that about?" Jude says. AJ and Ollie just

give me concerned looks.

"It was just a joke," I say. I force out a bark of laughter. "It's like, can he not take a joke?" Everyone looks at me, clearly not buying it.

"I guess, dude," says Jude. "Fresno's actually pretty sensitive, though. He seems chill but—you shouldn't say stuff like that to him."

"Whatever," I say. I can't look anyone in the eye. "I've gotta get home. I have stuff to do." I skate off without looking back. Nobody says anything as I leave. I want the ground to open up and swallow me. I manage to hold in my tears until I get to my room.

I barely leave my bed the next day. Every time I think about Fresno or my friends or skating at all, I feel a cringe so visceral that I have to curl up in the fetal position. This is the closest I've ever gotten to having real friends—to having *best* friends—and I blew the whole thing to shit. That's all I ever do.

I stay curled up under my comforter, rotting, until the next afternoon. Sometime after lunch there's a knock on my bedroom door. I figure it's my mom, so I don't look up when the door opens. When I hear Fresno clear his throat, I sit straight up. My body has a weird, weightless feeling like I'm in a dream.

"What's up?" he asks. I don't understand how he can be so chill in this situation. Personally, I'm about to have an anxiety attack. I didn't expect to see him again—especially not here, in my room. Why is he here? Does he want to get back at me for what I said? That doesn't seem like Fresno, but I'm too nervous to let go of the thought. Fear twists my stomach.

When I don't say anything, he sighs. "Yeah," he says, "I figured."

My consciousness is lodged somewhere deep in my guts, trying to hide. I hear myself ask, "Why are you here?" Fresno looks confused.

"I wanted to make sure you were okay," he says. "The other day you seemed . . . off. We were all worried." I stare at him, barely comprehending. I was a jerk to everyone and they all worried about me? I soften a little.

"I'm such a dick," I say, my voice a whisper. I glance at him, and the look of concern in his eyes is so intense it's hard to look at. I wrap my comforter around my shoulders and fix my eyes on the floor. "I'm always mean, even when I don't want to be. I don't know why I said that stuff to you," I say. Fresno sits down on the corner of my mattress.

"I don't think you're a dick," he says gently. I sigh.

"Well, you're wrong. Look at what's happening right now. I should be apologizing to you, not making this all about me." I feel the mattress dip as he turns to face me.

"I don't think you're making this all about you," he says. I roll my eyes.

"Of course you'd say that. You're too nice," I say.

"Sloane," he says, so firmly that I look up at him. He still looks concerned, but now there's a hint of hurt in his expression. "Don't act like I'm an idiot just because I'm not, like, the most aggro guy ever born. I know you can be rude, but I'm also worried about you." He huffs out a breath. "And it's not because I spend every waking moment being worried about everyone I meet because I'm just so *nice*. I'm worried about you because you're my friend and I care about you. You, in particular."

His chest rises and falls heavily, but he seems more nervous than angry. I blink at him. I've never heard Fresno talk for so long before. Something about his frustration pulls me to the surface of my anxiety, so I'm still treading water but I'm not drowning anymore. I always liked Fresno because he was so chill, so unbothered. I've never seen him get like this before. Everything slides off him so easily—or, I thought it did. But maybe I misunderstood. Maybe the things I thought were sliding off him were actually collecting inside him. Maybe there's a pit in his stomach where all the bad stuff goes to grow mold. There's a pit like that in mine.

"Sorry," I say after his breathing evens out.

"Sorry," he replies, "I didn't mean to go off. Was that weird?" We're facing each other, each of us with one leg dangling over the side of the bed. I reach out and gently kick his foot.

"Not weird," I say. "I get it." He gives me a small smile.

"Now I made this whole conversation about *me*," he says.

"Well, I like talking about you," I say. I feel myself blush.

"I like talking about you, too," he says. We are both quiet for a moment.

I look at him sitting there, with his worn-out jeans, his black-hole eyes, his slightly pigeon-toed feet, and I realize that we're in the same place. I mean, I realize I can see him more clearly than

I could before, like there's no shimmer between us, no cloud, no alternate dimension. He's my friend Fresno, and he cares about me even when I'm annoying, and he gets angry about things and feels things and says stuff he regrets. I've always felt like I was alone in my intensity, like nobody else was feeling things the way I was. But now I have Fresno with me. I know he's feeling the same overwhelming everything that I am. He can see me. He wants to see me.

I suddenly feel overwhelmed by the fact that he's here, in my room, on my bed. I reach out and shove him gently. He lets himself slide off the bed and fall to the ground.

"That was *not* swaggy," he says from the floor. I groan but I can't hold in my laugh. He smiles real big and starts laughing too, and for a while we just sit there, cracking up.

I decide to go to the skate park the next evening. I'm nervous, but I want to see my friends more than I'm nervous. Fresno and I are cool, but I don't know how everyone else is feeling. They're all hanging out by the half-pipe when I get there.

"Okay," Jude says to me as soon as I walk up. "Do you think whipped cream counts as a sauce?"

"*Some* of us think it does and *some* of us have bad opinions about everything anyway," says AJ, looking pointedly at Ollie.

"You can't say all my opinions are wrong just because I don't like *Mamma Mia*," Ollie says, exasperated.

"It sucks to hear you say that out loud," says Jude. AJ puts their head in their hands.

"ABBA is Swedish, why would their musical be set in Greece?" Ollie asks. Jude and AJ both start yelling at once. My nerves dissolve as I listen to them bicker. When I look over at Fresno, I see he's already looking at me. He nods his head and I follow him away from the group.

"They've been fighting for, like, ten minutes," he says, "I'm glad you're finally here." I feel my face flush. I notice he's blushing too.

It's weird that I haven't known Fresno forever. He's become such an integral part of my daily life. He and Jude and Ollie and AJ are the people I want to go to whenever something cool happens, whenever I land a new trick or do slightly above average on a science test or I find a potato chip that looks like Hatsune Miku. But they're also the people I want to go to when something shitty happens, when my mom threatens to ground me for skateboarding in the house or I get my period really bad or I have to eat the potato chip that looks like Hatsune Miku.

I didn't realize how much stuff happened to me on a daily basis until I had people to tell about it. It's like my life is totally full all the way up to the top. And when I get pushed into the other dimension really hard, they all know how to reach through the shimmery cloud and join me on the other side.

"Can I, like, actually show you how to do a kickflip now?" Fresno asks. I laugh.

"Please," I say. A breeze blows through the park. A crescent moon hangs overhead. In the yellow glow of the skate park lights, Fresno teaches me how to kickflip.

SKIN AND FUR

When I joined the horror movie club, I hoped it would help me find new friends. I saw a flyer for the club at the movie theater, and even though I'm not really a joiner-inner, I was tired of being alone and I figured this might be an easy way to meet people. Not like, *meet people* meet people. Just find some friends.

What it did instead was put me in a dark room with my ex-husband.

The horror movie club meets the first Monday of every month at the Cryptid Creek Cinema, the town's one-screen movie theater. It's the kind of movie theater I've always wanted to live near. According to the flyer, the club watches a movie together in the theater, then goes down the street to drink and chat at Screamin' Demon since they don't have karaoke on Mondays. This seemed low-effort enough for even someone like me. I can watch a movie and have a glass of wine. This is, in fact, the way

I spend most evenings anyway.

Cryptid Creek Cinema is a cool, retro theater. I walk through the domed atrium with its crystal chandelier and past the concession stand with vintage snack ads. The theater itself is pretty large, full of green velvet seats and a screen framed by classic red curtains. Pinprick lights on the ceiling shine like tiny stars.

Coming in here brings me instant relief. The air is cool and the seats are surprisingly comfortable. I like the quiet ticking sound of the old film projector and the murmurs of the crowd before a film starts. A very long time ago I'd tried to go to film school, but I gave up when my dream school rejected me.

I'm still standing in the entry of the theater when someone says my name.

"Griffin?" calls a deep, rough voice. My heart sinks. I look around until I see him, standing on the far side of the room. My ex-husband. And of course, he looks great. And of course, I'm wearing my backup glasses, the ones that never sit straight on my face and make me look wonky. I give him a half-hearted wave and he makes his way through the row of seats.

My ex-husband, Mitch, is crazy hot. It's an objective fact, one that I can admit even though I no longer have feelings for him. He's over a foot taller than me, broad-shouldered and strong, built like a cartoon lumberjack. His body is humanoid, but he has a wolf's head, with a snout and teeth and sharp yellow eyes. His dark brown fur is speckled with gray. Tonight, he's wearing a duster, trousers, T-shirt, and loafers, all in varying shades of brown. I've never understood why he feels the need to look so put-together all the time. It's like, we're at movie club. Just wear jeans.

"Hey, Mitch," I say when he stops in front of me. I haven't been this close to him in a long time. I feel a wave of emotions sweep over me. Anger, guilt, loss, sadness. I try to subtly run a hand through my hair and make sure my jacket collar isn't turned in like always.

"You look good," he says, eyeing me with a kind of appraisal that feels inappropriate, given our history. I clench my jaw, but deep down I feel a twinge of delight at being looked at like this. The feeling grows stronger when I notice he's wagging his tail a little. His tail never lies.

"You too," I say, trying to be cordial. He grins at me like he knows exactly how good he looks. I'm instantly annoyed.

"I didn't think you liked horror movies," he says. I roll my eyes.

"Classic of you to forget that I like something you also like," I say, the response more aggressive than I'd meant it to be. Mitch was always a big fan of horror movies, but he knew I was the film guy. He knew I enjoyed the occasional horror flick. He knew I loved *The Wicker Man* after he showed it to me. Was it really that surprising that I'd come to a horror movie club? Mitch raises his eyebrows.

"I didn't mean to offend you," he says.

"You didn't offend me," I snap, much too quickly to seem unoffended. It's so me to run into Mitch and immediately lose my cool. Nobody can piss me off faster than he can.

"Did you bring anyone with you?" he asks, trying to keep the conversation going. That's when I look around the room and realize we're the only two people who came alone. I think about telling him I brought someone, but it would be too obvious a lie. I shake my head resignedly. "Yeah, me neither," he says. We stand there for an uncomfortable moment. I can't tell what Mitch is thinking, but I'm a little offended he hasn't offered to sit with me. Mitch is the nice one, the one more likely to make the polite choice. I'm supposed to be the one who doesn't want to sit with him.

While I'm having this internal struggle, the lights dim. Mitch sits and gestures to the seat next to him, offering it to me. I pretend not to see and walk forward a few rows to sit next to a goth girl and a tall woman who seems to be made of metal.

"I'm sitting next to you because I'm avoiding my ex-husband," I whisper to the girl. This is what he's driven me to—actually talking to strangers. She looks up at me. Her eyes are lined with dark makeup.

"After the movie, you have to tell me everything about this," she whispers back. I laugh, surprised, and she smiles. Then the film begins.

I sit down at the bar with Theo and Flatwoods and order a very large glass of red wine.

"That's him?" Theo asks when I sneak a glance at Mitch. I blush at being caught looking, but I nod. Mitch is sitting at the far end of the bar, entertaining a group of people who already seem enamored with him. Theo and Flatwoods look at him, both trying—and failing—to be discreet. Then they both look back at me as if reevaluating.

"What?" I ask.

"Nothing," says Theo, at the same time that Flatwoods says "He's hot."

"But you're hot, too!" Theo interjects.

"In a different way," says Flatwoods. Theo shoots her a glare.

"Yeah, but still hot," Theo says. Flatwoods nods, although I know what she's thinking. It's what I assume everyone thinks when they see me and Mitch together: Why would someone as handsome and well-dressed and generally put-together as Mitch be with a guy like me? I mean, I have a certain charm that some people respond to. An ex once called me "character actor hot," which I think means I have a strong brow line and it's clear I broke my nose a few times. I think I make this work for me pretty well. But Mitch is on another level.

I look across the bar at him, at the cut of his jaw and his thick fur. He has an easy charm that radiates from him like heat, so I can feel it even all the way over here. Everything's always been easy for him.

Nobody will admit this, but it's harder dating in this town if you're human. The cryptids are all a little bored by us. Why settle for a human guy when you could date someone who's literally seven feet tall and has shoulders wider than your wingspan? I was shocked when Mitch first hit on me. Looking at him now,

I'm still a little shocked. But I guess it just makes everything that happened afterwards even more inevitable.

"Did you know he was going to be here tonight?" asks Theo. Flatwoods leans in.

"No," I say miserably, "I came here to get my own life, away from him." Theo pats me on the shoulder.

"How long ago did you break up?" she asks. I sigh.

"Six months ago. We were together for three years, but our marriage only lasted three months." Theo winces and Flatwoods makes a crackling static sound.

"What happened?" asks Flatwoods.

"You don't have to answer that," Theo quickly adds, although I can tell by her face that she really wants me to answer. I figure I might as well oblige. I take a long sip of my wine.

"Things were going well. We eloped. Everything fell apart," I say. Flatwoods and Theo look at me expectantly. I think about leaving it at that, but then I hear Mitch's laugh and I see him giving some bigfoot the same appraising look he gave me earlier. The wine in my stomach turns sour. "I don't know," I continue, "being married changed things. Which doesn't make any sense, because it didn't literally change anything. We were already living together and building a life together. But the word *married* freaked Mitch out. He's an ambitious guy. I think being married made him feel like he was stalled out or something." I take another sip, shooting a glance at Mitch to make sure he isn't overhearing this. "It wasn't a big dramatic thing. He just stopped being my partner. Stopped being interested in my life, stopped wanting to spend time with me. Then everything just stopped." I hear Mitch make a joke and all his new friends laugh. I flush with anger.

"Dude," says Theo compassionately.

"We'll hate him for you," says Flatwoods. That makes me chuckle.

"You don't have to hate him," I say.

Although, it doesn't exactly feel bad to have friends who hate Mitch. All my old friends were really Mitch's friends and they all stopped seeing me after the divorce. I've been so deeply alone the last six months. I've had a lot of time to think about how much I hate Mitch. But the worst thing about Mitch is, I can never completely hate him. There's still some speck of love left in my body, like a stain on an old T-shirt.

Mitch was always good at taking care of me when I was depressed. He'd make me food and rent some dumb movies and read to me. Simple things, but meaningful things. When I couldn't express how I was feeling, he wouldn't make me talk. He'd just cup his hands around my face and tuck a lock of hair behind my ear. He'd look at me and I'd know everything was okay. He made me happy in a way that nobody else ever had. Then, the divorce.

"Do you think you'll come to movie club again?" Theo asks.

"I'm not sure," I admit.

"You should, though!" she says. She places a hand on my shoulder, clearly a little tipsy. "You have to come back. We like hanging out with you," she says, and Flatwoods nods behind her. "And not just because you told us a bunch of good gossip. Although that didn't hurt." She laughs. Hearing that Theo and Flatwoods want to see me again has more of an effect on me than I'd care to admit.

"I'll think about it," I say. But I know I'll be back. I realize I'm smiling.

The next month passes mostly without note. I go on a few dates. I started dating immediately after the divorce, with the idea that "getting back out there" would help me somehow. So far, it has not helped. But I keep doing it. I want to meet someone who makes me completely forget about Mitch—not just about the divorce, but about Mitch himself.

I don't want to spend any more long nights remembering the warmth of his fur or the soft growl of his voice or the feeling of his claws on my skin. I don't want to turn the corner in the town house we shared and expect to see him standing in the kitchen, doing dishes. I don't want to think about how he made me feel like I was standing on solid ground for once in my life. I want to forget all of it, blow it up, erase it. I want to go on a date so good that it solves all of my problems and transforms me into the person I'm meant to be—someone with his shit together, someone who owns shoes other than sneakers, someone who doesn't get evil when he drinks red wine.

I haven't managed to find this magical date yet. I've just been on a bunch of deeply mediocre dates with deeply mediocre guys.

Have I been hooking up with them? Yes. Has the sex been middling to bad and left me feeling weirdly isolated and slightly insane? Yes. So I'm relieved when it's finally time for horror movie club again.

"Griffin!" Theo calls as soon as I walk in the theater door. She and Flatwoods wave and point out an empty seat next to them. As I walk down the aisle, I see Mitch watching me. He's sitting with his new friends, including that bigfoot I saw him checking out. He nods at me, and when I nod back he gives me that smile I hate so much. I look away quickly.

After the movie, I sit with Theo and Flatwoods at the bar and try to ignore Mitch, who seems to be trying to catch my eye. I notice he and the bigfoot are flirting more tonight. I wonder if they saw each other at all since last month. The bigfoot touches Mitch's bicep and I see his tail wag. I roll my eyes and feel a clench of frustration in my chest. After I point out the flirting to Theo and Flatwoods, we spend the rest of the night joking about it. I feel a little more okay than usual when I go home.

The next meeting is the same: trying to avoid Mitch, gossiping with Theo and Flatwoods. It isn't until the fourth meeting that something changes.

The something in question is Theo and Flatwoods's early departure from the bar. Theo was tired from work and Flatwoods wanted to take her home. I'm planning to finish my drink and then follow them when I feel someone slide into the seat next to me.

"Hey there," Mitch says when I turn to look at him. His low voice is nearly a growl. He's the only individual I know who can make a simple greeting sound so sexy. I try to push the word *sexy* out of my mind.

"Hi, Mitch," I say, trying to keep my voice as flat as possible.

"Is it okay if I sit here?" he asks. "I need a break from Cleo and Mothman's in-jokes." I look down the bar and see that Cleo and Mothman are indeed doing some kind of very involved bit that requires a lot of gesticulating and giggling, while Lucy rolls their eyes. I sigh.

"You can sit wherever you want. I was about to leave." I clearly still have about half a drink left in my glass. I try to subtly chug some of it.

"How've you been?" he asks after a beat of awkward silence. I snort.

"How do you think I've been?" I ask. I drank my wine too fast and now I'm feeling antagonistic. Mitch holds up his hands.

"My bad. I'll find somewhere else to sit," he says and starts to stand up.

"Wait," I say, before I can think better of it. As much as I don't want him here, I really do kind of want him here. He makes me angrier than anyone else can, but there's also something so reassuring about his presence. His dark, curly fur and his sharp, white teeth and his startling yellow eyes that always seemed to be looking right to the core of me. I may be drunker than I thought.

"How have . . . you been?" I ask. A small grin passes over his lips.

"Probably about the same as you," he says. His tone is sardonic but his eyes look sad.

"I find that hard to believe," I reply. His eyes flash, somehow turning an even brighter yellow than usual.

"I forgot what a dick you are when you drink red wine," he says. I take a long, slow sip and keep my eyes locked on his.

"You like it when I'm like this," I say when I finally set my glass down. This earns me a genuine smile, not the flirty one that I hate so much but the surprised grin he reserves for when he's really pleased.

I'm not stupid—I know I can be a bitch. But that was always something that Mitch liked about me. He's such a goody-goody himself, I think he felt like he was living vicariously through me when I talked shit. My favorite memories with him are the times when I managed to drag him down to my level. He could be even meaner than me when he wanted to be, and it was exhilarating to see him like that. There was a rawness, an honesty to that version of him that I didn't see in his day-to-day persona.

He puts his arm on the bar and rests his cheek on his furry hand.

"Why is it hard to believe that I've been having a hard time?" His tone is genuine. The sincerity of his question catches me off guard.

"Because you're never having a hard time," I say. "You always have friends and you always have plans and you always look good." He cocks his head.

"You have friends, too. What about that couple you're always hanging out with? Theo and Flatwoods?"

"You're right, I have two whole friends," I say. I drum my fingers on the bar irritably. He rolls his eyes.

"Okay, so I'm more social. That doesn't mean I'm—"

"Have you been on any dates?" I interrupt. I can't make eye contact with him. It's a question that I do and don't want to know the answer to. He sighs.

"I don't want to talk about this with you," he says. He takes a sip of his beer. His ears are angled back, like he's annoyed.

"So you have been on dates?" I say, unable to help myself. The idea of him going out with other guys makes my skin crawl. It's a visceral, physical reaction—more potent than I expected.

He puts down his beer slowly and looks me in the eyes. Then he does something I didn't expect. He reaches out and tucks a lock of hair behind my ear. I'm too stunned to react, the sensation of his claw dragging across my skin sets my whole body on fire. He stands up and walks out of the bar without looking back at me.

I wake up the next morning feeling emotionally hungover. I sit up in bed and the memory of my conversation with Mitch pours back into me. I put my face in my hands. Mitch was trying to have a normal, adult conversation and I acted like a child. I wanted him to think that I was over it, that I was cool, calm, collected, whatever. I definitely didn't want him to think that I was spiraling out on the idea that he *might* be going on dates. I have to do something to fix this. I get dressed and go to Javalope to grab a coffee.

I order my and Mitch's preferred drinks from Mothman and head over to Mitch's place. I haven't actually seen his new apartment and I wonder what it will be like to see a space that's only his.

I find his name on the apartment buzzer and ring the bell. I hear his door open and his footsteps come down the stairs. It isn't early but it's still morning, and when he comes into view he's wearing a robe and slippers. He stops when he sees me standing at the door and seems to have an internal argument with himself about whether to let me in.

Finally, he opens the door. He stands so his body fills the doorway.

"To what do I owe this pleasure?" he asks. His ears are back like he's ready for a fight. I hold up the coffee.

"I brought you a cortado," I say. He sniffs the air and then looks at me, his yellow gaze going straight through me. I shiver. He moves out of the doorway and I follow him upstairs.

The first thing that strikes me about his apartment is how good it smells. A mix of his warm, earthy cologne and clean laundry and the green scent of the cleaning products he likes to use. The apartment is nearly spotless, the furniture nicely mismatched, the decor minimal and tasteful.

"Sorry for the mess," he says, gesturing at a cardigan that lays across the back of the couch. "I didn't expect to be hosting."

I knew he was neat, but I didn't realize he was *this* neat. When we lived together, the vibe of the town house was always "gay eclectic," which is to say it was packed full of all my little random trinkets. It must have been difficult to live with someone as mess-prone as me, but he never complained. He did, however, do more than his share of the chores.

"Your place looks great," I say. I put our coffee down on the little reclaimed-wood coffee table. "Very queer eye for the wolf guy." He smiles without looking at me. We sit down on the couch and I take a nervous sip of my Americano.

"I wanted to apologize about last night," I say. I thought about how to handle this when I was ordering our coffee and I settled on apologizing. Apologies always seem very mature. Mitch glances at me and then away. "I was a dick. There was no reason for me to act like that," I continue. Mitch nods. He's quiet, his brow furrowed like he's thinking hard.

"Sometimes you talk to me like I don't have feelings," he says. The expression on his face is pained and there's a heaviness to the slump of his shoulders. His left ear twitches, a nervous tic of his. I feel a pang of genuine remorse. Mitch is such a closed-off guy in so many ways. I know what it took for him to admit something like this. My whole agenda for coming here suddenly feels painfully trite.

"Is it okay that I came here?" I ask. I hadn't really expected to have this kind of conversation with Mitch again. As painful as it is to hear that I hurt him, I realize I'm also quietly grateful to be here with him. Mitch sighs and scratches his face.

"I think neither of us is very good at boundaries," he says. "Or at least, that's what my therapist thinks."

"You're seeing a therapist?" I ask. He nods.

"Since before we broke up, actually. I didn't tell you because you didn't seem to want to hear me talk about anything."

Something twists in my chest. I figure I might as well ask the questions I've been wanting to ask.

"Was I—" I take a deep breath. "Was I a bad husband?"

Mitch stares at his claws.

"Being married made me feel trapped." He glances at me to see my reaction. It hurts to hear him say it, but there's also something like relief floating just below the surface of the hurt. I could guess at what happened, at why he left me, but I never really knew. Now I know. He must see some anguish in my face, because he hurries to finish his explanation.

"Not because I wanted to be with anyone else. It just felt like an ending, somehow. And it seemed like marriage made you shut down. It was like you were on autopilot. I didn't know how to interact with you when you were like that."

I chew on my lip. He might have a point. I told myself I was just reacting to the distance he created, but maybe we both started acting weird at the same time. Maybe we couldn't just blame each other for everything we did wrong.

"I never wanted to break up," I say, my voice catching in my throat. The admission surprises us both. His ears perk up.

"You prefer being in relationships," he says.

"I didn't—first of all, you're not my therapist," I say, and he gives a small nod. "And what I meant was, I never wanted to break up with *you*."

Mitch finally looks me in the eyes. "I didn't want to break

up with you, either," he says. We stare at each other like we're trying to read each other's minds.

"Then why aren't we together now?" I ask quietly.

"You're dismissive of me," Mitch says. I wince, but he continues. "You care about me but you don't think about me enough."

"You never take anything seriously," I say. I feel sad and hurt and relieved and liberated all at once. "You're always trying to improve me in ways I don't want to be improved."

"You act like I'm going to fix everything for you whenever you have a problem," he says.

"You do fix everything for me when I have a problem," I say.

"We want different things," he says. I shake my head. The muddle of emotions that's been building up inside me since the divorce suddenly sharpens into a knifepoint of clarity.

"I want you," I say.

"I want you, too," he growls. And then we're on each other, skin and fur and nails and claws and his hot breath on every inch of me. I forgot how much he can do with his tongue. I yank off his robe and he pulls off my clothes and we half fuck, half fight each other on the floor of his living room.

I pour every ounce of resentment for him into my movements. I tug hard at his fur, push him onto his stomach, twist his arm behind his back until he keens in a combination of pain and pleasure. In return, he's desperate for me, begging for me, giving me everything I want so he can get what he needs. It is, to be frank, the best sex we've ever had. We fuck until we're both of out of breath, sweaty and panting on his tasteful area rug.

We lay there and I run a finger over his snout. His eyes are closed and he's still breathing heavily. He's so impossibly handsome. His dark, curly fur and his pointed ears and his broad shoulders and strong arms. I missed touching all of him. I missed being touched by him. But for the first time, I'm not really sure if I miss being married to him. Maybe we're better as whatever this is than we are as husbands.

"Where does this leave us?" he asks as if reading my mind. I tap my nail against one of his fangs.

"I guess it means we can sit together at movie club," I say. He laughs. His tail wags. Then he rolls on top of me and I'm too far gone to have any more coherent thoughts.

DREAM GIRL

Sas ran a hand through the tangle of hair that kept falling into his eyes. Whenever he did projects that didn't require his goggles, his hair got in his eyes. He was always making mental notes to keep more barrettes in his pockets, but he had a notoriously bad memory. So he had to deal with a lot of little things like this—cold cups of coffee, missing keys, backlogs of paperwork. He kept his workshop incredibly neat not because cleanliness was particularly meaningful to him, but because putting his tools back in the same place every day ensured that he would always be able to find them.

At this moment, he knew that his nails were arranged by size in a series of coffee cans by the door, his hammers were hung up on a pegboard by the window, and the first three drawers of his green work cart were full of different grits of sandpaper. He also knew that he was low on shop paper because he'd moved the roll by the front door instead of leaving it hanging below the

Sas

shelves. He had many such rituals and repetitions to ensure that his life operated as smoothly as possible.

Sas stood and brushed sawdust off his sleeveless flannel shirt. He pulled the bandana off his mouth and retied it around his neck. He had a small apartment at the back of the workshop, but he didn't feel like cooking tonight. He'd go pick up food from somewhere, probably the sandwich shop on the corner where he got dinner a few nights a week. He sighed, feeling overwhelmed with boredom at his routine. He pushed open the front door—and stopped short in the doorway, surprised to see someone on his doorstep, her hand raised as though she had been about to knock.

"Sorry," she said, looking up at him. Sas stared at her. He recognized this woman from around town. She owned the karaoke bar, Screamin' Demon, a place he hadn't been but had often passed. He couldn't remember her name—it was something simple, just on the tip of his tongue.

"I'm June," she said. She stuck out her hand to him.

"Sas," he said, shaking her hand.

"Yeah, I know," she said, giving him a coy grin. "I need some carpentry help and I hear you're the guy to ask."

Even from this deep in his emotional funk, Sas could see that June was stunning. Her hair was long and peach pink. Deep dimples emphasized her gap-toothed smile. Her round face was sprinkled with a little constellation of beauty marks. Her tank top and purple tennis skirt showed off her curves in a way that was somehow both casual and nearly indecent. She was maybe the hottest person he'd ever seen.

"Well," she said, a look of uncertainty crossing her face for the first time, "maybe you don't have time to help? I should've called first." Sas realized he'd been staring at her silently for just long enough to make it weird.

"Oh," he said, nervously pulling at the fur on the back of his hand. "No, you're fine. I have time for you." June smiled, the uneasiness slipping off her face. Did she have a little gemstone on her left canine? He felt faint. "You can come in if you want," he said, and stepped out of the doorway so June could enter.

It was funny seeing her in his space. His workshop was clean, bordering on austere, and June was the opposite. She was a bright point of light, a little pink disco ball turning in the center of the room, taking everything in.

"You run the karaoke bar, right?" he asked. She sighed.

"Ugh. Yes. I mean, I love it. But, ugh," she said, shaking her head. "There's always some big problem to solve. I finally got a new speaker to replace the one that's always making a hissing sound, and now I have to replace part of the stage. I love that the swamp monsters love karaoke so much, but they're so damp that a hole started rotting through the wood."

"So you want me to fix your stage?" he asked. She looked up at him, dark eyelashes over dark eyes, a nervous crease between her eyebrows.

"Could you?" she asked.

"I mean, technically I mostly make furniture, but I can probably fix anything so long as it's wood. I'm, uh, handy," he said.

He held up a hand, watched June take in the size of it. Her eyes grew large and her round cheeks flushed. Sas felt a shiver of pleasure run down his spine.

"Yes," she said, a little too quickly. She cleared her throat and said, more calmly this time, "That would be great." He ran his hand over the back of his neck.

"How about if you come by sometime soon so you can see the problem and we can go over details? When are you free?" June asked.

He answered without thinking: "Tomorrow," he said. "I'm free tomorrow." For a second he was nervous that this made him seem desperate, but when June smiled so big that he could see the gem on her tooth, he didn't feel nervous anymore.

"I'm free tomorrow too," she said. "Want to come by tomorrow morning? Around nine?"

"It's a date," he said. That gem again, winking from the corner of her smile. That perfect blush spreading across her cheeks.

"Can't wait," she said. She spun on her heel and practically skipped out the door. He wasn't sure if the skipping was due to excitement or because June was just the kind of person who tended to skip. He watched her until she turned the corner out of sight, and then he finally went back inside his apartment. The workshop looked a little bigger than it did before she arrived.

The next morning, Sas spent longer in front of his bathroom mirror than he had in a long time. He'd been rotating the same three or four outfits every day for the last few months. His wardrobe was mostly cutoff flannel, T-shirts for obscure punk bands, and thrifted jeans. He knew he wasn't exactly reinventing the butch wheel with any of these looks, but they were comfortable and good to work in. Today, though, he wanted to look good.

He put on the well-worn blue-and-white striped mechanic coveralls that made him look like the biggest slut at the auto body repair shop. He rolled up the sleeves and unzipped the collar a tasteful amount, and then he unzipped a little more. He made sure that a curlicue of hair was laid nicely on his furry forehead. He was covered in fur but he liked to keep the fur on his head a little longer, a little more styled. He checked the clock and realized he was supposed to be at the karaoke bar in a few minutes.

With one last glance in the mirror, Sas hurried out the door. Screamin' Demon was only a few blocks away, but he still rushed down the street. He didn't want to keep June waiting. When he arrived at the bar, he took a second to compose himself before he opened the front door.

Inside, the place was all glitter. Even with most of the lights off, he could tell that basically every surface was coated in glitter. The ceiling was completely covered in disco balls of every size. The walls were pink—everything was pink—and behind the stage was a big neon sign that said *Screamin' Demon*. The whole place looked like if a pop song exploded. But, like, a really good pop song.

Sas was looking around in awe when June popped up from

behind the bar.

"You're here!" she said, shooting him a wide smile and coming around the corner. Today her pink hair was tied up in a long ponytail and she was wearing hot-pink bike shorts and an oversized Sailor Moon T-shirt. Sas had to force himself to look away from her legs in those bike shorts. He had a thing for thick thighs. Or maybe it wasn't a thing specific to him, but just a consequence of being alive. Either way, he was definitely looking at her face right now.

"I'm here," he said, unable to think of a better response. He was unable to think of anything, really, surrounded as he was by June and her glitter. She clapped her hands together and he mentally shook himself.

"Okay! Let me show you what the problem is," she said, and led him over to the stage. The karaoke bar wasn't a huge space. There was just enough room for a stage and a bar and a bit of seating. The low stage took up a quarter of the bar. It was (unsurprisingly) covered in a layer of pink carpeting.

June bent over to peel the carpet back. Sas watched her do it. Her bike shorts were *so* tight. It had been a while since Sas had been this attracted to someone. The dyke dating scene in the Creek was solid for a town this size, but it sometimes felt a bit small for a seven-foot-tall, generally unkempt, often depressed butch lesbian who used he/him pronouns. Sas found himself getting a little bored of it—as he'd been bored with most things in his life recently. There were only so many times he could hook up with his ex, or his ex's ex. Sas liked the excitement of something new, and while he loved this town, there wasn't a lot of new. But there was, apparently, June.

June wasn't really his usual type; he tended to go for alt girls, mediocre drummers, girls who smoked cloves, hand-poke tattoo artists. Those kinds of women were his bread and butter. He knew what kind of dates they'd want to go on, what they'd want to talk about, how they would want to be kissed. It was reassuring to have that kind of certainty. He didn't know what someone like June would want. He wanted to find out.

She pointed to a dark spot on the wood of the stage.

"That's a problem, right?" she asked, tapping it with the toe of her sneaker. Sas was glad to have something besides June to focus on. He took a step closer so he could inspect the spot. It was definitely water damaged, not to the point of being dangerous but on its way there.

"I might need to rebuild the whole front of the stage," he said finally. "It'll probably take a few days." June tugged on the end of her ponytail.

"How much will it cost?" she asked.

"Just pay me for materials," Sas told her. Her brow furrowed and she started to object, but he interrupted. "It's the cute girl discount." She blushed furiously at this and he could see her trying to suppress a smile. He gave her his best lazy grin, the one where a few of his sharp teeth were visible.

"At least let me give you free drinks," she said. He agreed and they shook on it. She had soft hands.

He grabbed his toolbox from where he'd left it next to the

door. June stood a little awkwardly by the bar and watched him set up. Normally he worked alone. He liked the quiet, the time he spent solely with the project. But today, almost without thinking about it, he turned to June and asked, “If I take measurements, could you write them down for me?” She beamed and hurried over to him to take the notebook and pen. When he saw how big she smiled, he was happy he asked her to help. He set down his toolbox and got to work.

As he took measurements of the stage, he kept finding himself distracted by June. Usually working pulled him into a place of deep focus, but today he couldn’t keep his attention on the job. He couldn’t stop noticing her. It was even harder once he clocked that she was noticing him quite a lot as well. At first he tried to convince himself that she was just watching him work, but the more he caught her looking, the harder it was to convince himself that her gaze was casual.

He felt flattered, panicked, giddy, overwhelmed. It had been a long time since he’d felt this way about a girl’s attention. He started to panic: Did June even know he was a lesbian? She might be straight, might think he was a guy, might be uninterested in him if she knew who he was. Even in a town as diverse and open-minded as Cryptid Creek, he was the only he/him dyke currently out. He tensed as the thought crossed his mind. He needed to make sure June was on the same page.

“I guess I’m kind of a lesbian stereotype,” he said. June blinked at him and he realized that he’d spoken very loudly into a room that had been silent for more than a few minutes. He could feel his hand growing sweaty around the tape measure. "You know, because of the carpentry," he added. June smiled in a friendly, uncertain way. He could feel his anxiety beginning to spiral and he tried to think of something to say that would recover the vibe.

"I was thinking you were a lesbian stereotype because you're a butch bigfoot. You know how there's so many butch lesbian bigfoots out there," June said with a grin. Sas stared at her. His mind was a nervous mess and it took him a minute to process what she'd just said. As it clicked through the rusty gears of his brain, he gave her a big smile full of relief.

"We really need to unionize," he said. June giggled and a bolt of pleasure shot through him. He got back to work, but now he was even more aware of her eyes on him.

He bent down with his tape measure, and out of the corner of his eye he saw her staring at his ass. He rolled up his sleeves and she bit her lip. He reached for something and her eyes traced the long line of his body, her dark lashes heavy over her eyes. He had to measure everything three times to make sure he was getting the right numbers. The fact of June's interest filled the room.

Finally, after taking twice as long as usual to do this simple task, Sas packed up his toolbox. His body was buzzing from June's attention. They had never gotten particularly near to each other, but he felt like he'd spent the afternoon entwined with her. She watched him so closely, with such hunger in her eyes. And Sas hadn't tried to keep his interest hidden, either. He'd watched her right back. There was an intimacy in this exchange that he hadn't often felt. An even give and take. He closed his toolbox and stood.

"I guess I'll just . . ." He hitched a thumb toward the door. June looked stricken.

"Oh, sure," she said. They both stood quietly for a moment, pointedly not looking at each other. Suddenly, her eyes lit up. "Oh! You have to come by tonight when we're actually open. So I can make you a drink," she said. Sas hesitated. He hadn't gone out in a while, hadn't drunk in a while—he supposed he hadn't been doing much of anything the past few months. It might be good to try something new.

"I'll be here," he said, before he could change his mind. June's face broke into a smile. It was stupid how pretty she was. They said goodbye again, and this time Sas actually left. He realized when he got back to his apartment that he was smiling.

Sas debated for a long time whether he should change clothes or wear the same outfit. In the end he settled on a black T-shirt and a pair of black jean shorts. He put on a gold chain and small gold hoop earrings to make the outfit a little nicer. It felt good to spend time on himself, to remember that he was hot. He grinned at his reflection and his teeth looked sharp and white. He walked out the door.

The bar was already busy when he walked in. He spotted Mothman and his partner sitting in one of the pink velvet booths making eyes at each other. The music was loud and upbeat, a synthy pop song that Sas had never heard but already liked. June waved as he walked up to the bar. He squeezed in next to a dogman and his date.

"You made it!" June said. Her face was already red from the heat of the room. "You look cute," she said. Her tone was so light and friendly that Sas couldn't tell if this was a flirty compliment or a regular compliment. Either way, he sat up a little straighter on his barstool.

"What should I order?" he asked.

"I'm gonna make you a gin pom," June said, already turning away from him to grab the ingredients. He felt a thrill down his back. There was something deeply sexy about June telling him what to do. Also, he liked gin. June turned to him and began making his drink.

"This is my specialty," she said. "I pretty much opened this bar to make gin poms and watch people do karaoke." She laughed at herself as she poured him a peachy pink drink. Sas laughed too.

"I got into carpentry because I like the smell of sawdust," he said, surprising himself with this admission. It made June giggle. He felt a thrill at the sound, at the way she scrunched her nose, at the way her dimples deepened. She handed him his drink. He took it, appreciating the cool feel of the condensation.

"Okay, take a sip! I want to know what you think!" June urged. Her dark eyes were locked on him as he lifted the glass to his lips. The flavor was sugary and biting, with a tart sweetness of pomelo juice and an intense juniper from the gin. Sas knew he seemed like the kind of guy who would take his liquor neat, but he'd always preferred a fun drink. Something sweet and fruity and brightly colored, maybe even a little bubbly; something he had to sip slowly because otherwise he'd be hungover before he even finished drinking it. The drink June had given him was exactly what he liked. It was also strong as hell.

"Powerful stuff," he said. June smiled. He took another sip. Somehow this one hit him even harder than the first. "Very powerful," he said, clearing his throat. He was already feeling a tipsy warmth spilling into his chest.

"That's why I like it," June said. "I like drinks that feel like they're trying to knock you out." He loved that June loved this kind of drink. He loved that it was the same color as her hair. He could sit here and watch her make drinks all night.

Someone walked up to the other end of the bar and June flitted away. Sas thought about how happy he was to be so close to June. Maybe she actually liked him. Maybe he could give himself permission to have a crush on her without fearing rejection.

Sas sipped his drink and watched her work the room. In one smooth movement, she would take a drink order from a swamp monster, turn to a cute girl and compliment her makeup, make a drink for a chupacabra, collect a few tips, give everyone her brightest smile, flip her hair over her shoulder, cheer at the end of a karaoke song, wipe up a spilled vodka cran. And every time she smiled at someone, she made it feel like she was smiling only at them, like this was a special, particularly incandescent smile that she reserved especially for them. She was so good at this, at talking to people and giggling at the right times and creating these little champagne bubbles of intimacy, short-lived and delicate and sparkling.

As Sas watched her, he grew simultaneously more impressed and more anxious. He loved that she was so good at this. He was realizing, however, that it was June's job to flirt with people. Had she actually been flirting with him, or was she just like that? Sometimes when he spent too long working on a project, he'd get stuck in carpenter mode and he'd only be able to see the world in joinery and angles. Maybe June spent so much of her day flirting that she could never really turn it off. His drink took on a sour edge.

The rest of the night went on like this, Sas sitting at the bar slowly sipping his gin pom, watching the other patrons drink and dance and laugh and kiss. Watching June fill drinks and smile at everyone who came up to the bar. He left when her back was turned.

The cool night air sobered him up a bit. He realized how silly he had been to assume that June liked him. He was too introverted for someone as outgoing as her. Blushing a few times and giggling at him didn't mean she was actually into him. He was a serious guy, a workaholic who had often been described as aloof. He and June had nothing in common.

It wasn't until he was nearly home that he realized his keys weren't in his pocket. He froze on the sidewalk, feeling the familiar sinking sensation that accompanied his frequent lapses in memory. Now he remembered unclipping his carabiner from his belt loop so he could fidget with it nervously while June flitted around the bar. He must have set it down on the bar without thinking. He sighed heavily. This was why he didn't like to deviate from his routine.

The thought of returning to Screamin' Demon was daunting, but he had to do it. He needed his keys to get back into his apartment. Slowly, begrudgingly, he turned around and made his way back to the bar. The walk was only a few blocks, but it felt far.

As soon as he stepped back inside, June caught his eye. She smiled, but something about the smile didn't feel quite genuine.

"Forget something?" she asked, and held up his carabiner. He nodded sheepishly and walked up to the bar. He mumbled an apology and she handed over his keys. She looked a little . . . definitely not angry, but not happy either. He didn't know her well enough to unpack her expression. Cautious, maybe. He felt some distance between them that hadn't been there before. He thanked her and turned to leave again.

"Bye, Sas," she called from the bar. He looked over his shoulder and saw that the expression he couldn't read seemed deeper than before. He wasn't sure how to fix this, or what he'd done wrong. He gave her a small wave and walked out the door.

He was relieved when he got back to his apartment. It was so nice to open the door and see his meticulously organized home, to know that everything was exactly where he had put it. At least here there would be no surprises. No threat of something new. Briefly, he conjured the image of June standing in middle of the room, her interest lighting up every corner. He shook his head, banishing the image.

The next day, he went back to Screamin' Demon to do his job. He wouldn't get distracted by thoughts of June and her likely nonexistent interest in him. He would try not to worry about whatever it was that had happened last night. He would stay in the little wooden box of himself.

At first, this was relatively easy. Sas's favorite part of carpentry was the beginning, when he was sawing and hammering and drilling something into being. He liked feeling the rough wood grow smooth in his hands, feeling the heat from the power tools. This was the part of the process where he felt the most productive, the most like he was truly making something from scratch. He managed to focus for a while. But eventually, June broke through his concentration.

She was quieter than usual. While he worked, she mostly focused on cleaning the bar. She only asked him a few questions, only made a few comments. She was reserved. And even when she was being reserved, Sas couldn't stop paying attention to her. Her silence took up as much space in his head as her words. He couldn't handle being so close to her and not getting to interact with her. "Can I ask you something?" Sas asked as he lowered his dust mask. June looked up at him, surprised.

"Of course," June said.

"How do you do your job?" he asked. She tilted her head, confused.

"Like, how do I make drinks?" she asked. He shook his head.

He stopped what he was doing to look at her.

"No, like, how do you do the customer part? How do you spend every night interacting with so many people and being so friendly to everyone?" Unexpectedly, she sighed. Her shoulders slumped and her face suddenly looked very tired. Sas was a little alarmed. "I didn't mean to—" he started, but she interrupted him.

"No, you're fine. It's a good question. I guess I don't really know how I do it," she said. She ran a hand through her hair, swept it all up in a ponytail and then let it fall loose against her back. "I love being around people and making them happy, but it gets exhausting. Sometimes I want to kick everyone out and close early and never open up again." She sighed and groaned at the same time. "But also, this really is my favorite place and some nights I never want to close, I just want to keep everyone around until the sun comes up and then we can all hang out forever and we'll never be alone," she said, giving Sas a sheepish grin.

"I don't know what I'd do if I was never alone," he said. He pictured his workshop filled with people, people who all needed something from him and never wanted to leave. The idea gave him a headache. June was watching him closely, her expression once again unreadable.

"I wish I was better at doing what you do," he said quietly. A moment of silence passed. They didn't look at each other, but somehow Sas could feel June's mind on him. He could feel her running him over in her head. He did the same to her. The bar felt a little smaller, a little more familiar.

"Thanks for saying that," she said finally. She smiled, a hint of fatigue still lingering on her face. Sas went back to work, but June was quieter now, her demeanor less perky. She didn't seem upset; she seemed comfortable. Sas sank into the feeling, letting it wash over him. He kept working on the stage.

That night at the bar, he watched June closely. Her charisma was even more impressive now that he understood the work that went into it. And yet, she still seemed completely at ease. If he didn't know she was worn out, he never would have noticed. Even knowing, he still didn't see signs of exhaustion. June simply didn't stop. He spent the night admiring her. He didn't once fall into his usual spiral of self-doubt. His whole brain was taken up with thoughts of June. He felt a roil of heat in his stomach at watching her be so completely in her element.

Whenever June had a free moment, she would turn the full power of her glittering charm directly on him. A fizzy warmth swept through him whenever she looked in his eyes; the feeling was dazzling, intoxicating. Instead of worrying about whether she was really flirting with him, he gave himself over to the feeling. He sipped his gin pom and melted a little every time she looked at him.

Toward the end of the night, when the crowd was thinning, he caught her standing at the far end of the bar looking absently at him. Like he was the place where her eyes naturally fell, like her gaze was drawn to him without her even noticing. When he made eye contact with her she blinked and quickly looked away.

Blush darkened her cheeks. Sas finished his drink. When he left that night, he made sure to say goodbye.

After the second to last day of work on the Screamin' Demon stage, Sas sat at the bar as usual. June wore red fishnets and a glittery pink dress that barely came down to her mid-thigh. He watched June and her sparkling smile and her fishnets. In the five days it had taken him to rebuild her stage, he'd gone from lovestruck to lovesick to heartbroken to something else. The something else felt less fragile than a crush, less fleeting than butterflies in his stomach. It felt rich and complex and substantial. In their long conversations during the day and long nights together at the bar, they had developed an intimacy that Sas hadn't experienced before. He was dreading tomorrow, when he'd finish up the stage and have no more excuse to spend endless time with June.

Sas didn't realize how late it had gotten until June announced last call. The bar started to empty until eventually only the two of them were left. They were deep in a conversation about something—Pokémon maybe, or French movies. Sas lost track every time June giggled.

When the last customer left, June came out from behind the counter to sit on the stool next to him. She flipped her hair over her shoulder and rested one leg on the bottom rung of his barstool.

"Come here often?" she asked. He grinned.

"Only when the hot bartender is working," he said. He felt

the pleasant warmth of several cocktails in his chest. A week ago, he couldn't have imagined saying something so bold to her. But now he knew she liked when he fed her corny one-liners. She giggled and leaned in, brushing a hand against his bicep. Sas caught her hand as she dropped it from his arm. It was small and warm and soft, her nails sharp and painted with tiny strawberries. He held her hand loosely, running a thumb over her knuckles. They sat like this, holding hands, looking at each other, for a while.

"Should we test out the stage?" June asked after a moment. Sas gave her hand a squeeze.

"You don't trust my handiwork?" he asked, teasingly. But he stood and led her to the stage, still holding her hand. June stepped up and paced across the new boards.

"Feels good to me," she said as she walked back to Sas.

"I aim to please," he said. June was standing on the edge of the stage while he stood on the floor, but even with the extra foot of height she only came up to his chest.

It took Sas a minute to realize they were leaning toward each other, getting closer and closer. He looked down at her, her eyes warm and brown behind thick lashes. It didn't occur to him to be nervous. He couldn't think about anything except June and the feeling of her hand in his.

It was almost miraculous how much Sas liked June. Everything about her was—not just appealing, but intoxicating. Her cherry perfume, her knife-sharp eyeliner, the gem in her canine, the shape of her, the way she held herself, the way she dressed.

Her body was a miracle and the fact that he got to be so near her body was a miracle. Her talent for making people happy was a miracle. Her ability to move through the world in exactly the way she wanted was a miracle. The fact that she wanted to spend so much time with him, that she raked her eyes over him whenever she thought he wasn't looking, the way she leaned forward to talk to him from across the bar. The way that being with her took him completely outside of himself, gave him a break from his overthinking and anxiety. When Sas was with June, his whole being was with her.

She reached a hand up, tenderly resting it on Sas's cheek. Sas was suddenly overwhelmed by the urge to kiss her. June's eyes flashed to his eyes, then to his lips, and he saw desire in her gaze. He lost it then. He slammed his lips into hers, his hands in her hair, tongue running against her teeth. She tangled her fingers into Sas's fur and bit down on his lip hard enough that he gasped into her mouth. Sas moved his hands to her waist, then swooped his arms around her and lifted her off the stage. She wrapped her legs around his waist.

Sas's mind was gone at this point. Holding June, all of her, feeling her weight against him, was a singular experience. She was sweet perfume and a tangle of pink hair. She was so completely June and she was so completely his in this moment. He traced a finger down her leg, the strings of her fishnets popping apart as it passed. June moaned and he paused. He waited until she looked at him, her eyelashes low over her eyes. Still making eye contact, he ran a finger down June's other leg. June gasped as each thread broke, and with each gasp Sas was pulled deeper into his own hunger.

When the last thread broke, he slowly laid June down on the stage, then knelt over her. He leaned down to kiss her, slower than before but more deeply. His thumb traced the top of June's skirt and she shivered. Sas continued to run his hand along the hem of her skirt. Her tights hung in tatters.

Her breath had become heavy and ragged. He watched her, eyes flicking to her chest occasionally as it heaved up and down. He moved his thumbs toward the space between her legs and she bit her lip. He paused and stared directly into her eyes.

"Tell me you want this," he said, his voice a low rasp. June's pupils were blown wide, her mouth swollen from kissing. She looked perfect. He watched as she struggled to find words.

"I want this," she said breathily, "I want you." A sharp pang of desire shot through Sas's body. It was almost painful, almost bittersweet. He grinned at June and she smiled back. The room around them was a glittery pink-and-neon blur. He and June were floating in their own little bubble. He leaned in and kissed her again, and his hand slipped up her skirt.

He rested his free hand on the stage next to June's head. There was a loud crack and his hand went through the board. June's moan turned to a startled yelp and she rolled away from the sound. Sas swore and pulled his hand from the newly formed hole in the stage. He was a little scratched but otherwise okay. June lay at his side, her eyes wide.

"How did that happen?" she asked. Sas felt his face grow hot.

He cleared his throat nervously.

"I might have, uh, forgotten to tighten a bolt on one of the supports," he mumbled, peering into the hole. He glanced at June and saw she was looking at him incredulously. "I told you I mostly build furniture," he said. "I've never built a stage before." He was aware that his tone was more defensive than it needed to be, but he couldn't help it.

He and June stared at each other for a long moment. Then, June's serious expression cracked and she smiled. She started laughing. At the sound of her laugh, he couldn't help but laugh too. And at the sight of her lying there giggling, her pink hair spread out around her, her fishnets ripped and hanging loosely around her legs, he couldn't help but lean in and kiss her. And he knew he wouldn't ever forget the way her lips felt on his as she laughed and kissed him back.

DUMB LITTLE CRUSH

Leaves brushed my face as I wandered through the plant store, Moonseed. Branches grazed my arms like they were reaching out for me. Plants overflowed from every available surface. There were succulents and cacti in watercolor greens and purples and pinks, and fig trees with leaves dark and shining. I hadn't considered before that there were *so* many shades of green. The shop was so wild and lush that there was something almost prehistoric about it. I felt like I'd stepped into a completely different place from the sunny summer day outside.

Today was my day off from Bookwraith and it was so nice out that I decided to spend the day just wandering around town. I hadn't been to Moonseed before because I'm a notorious plant killer. It's never on purpose, I just worry about my plants too much and then I overwater them and then they die. Lucy says I smother them because my unconscious need for control turns my instinct for care into accidental tyranny. I think Lucy should consider themself lucky that they're not the one getting smothered.

Today, though, I decided to make the leap and check out the plant store. The sun was shining and the sky was blue and it was just barely too hot. I could ignore my personal failings and imagine that I was the type of girl who had zero plant-related emotional baggage. At the very least, I could buy flowers. It would be so romantic to walk around today with an armful of beautiful flowers wrapped in brown paper. That was who I wanted to be today: the girl carrying the beautiful bouquet on a sunny day. That was a simple enough goal.

From the outside, Moonseed is just a lot of very fogged-up windows. But inside, as I was discovering, it was a dense forest of houseplants. I was admiring a monstera with leaves bigger than my head when I heard an odd clattering sound from the back of the shop. I moved deeper into the store, looking for the source of the noise. I jumped when I heard the clattering again, but much louder and much closer.

"Sorry," said a voice from behind an enormous Christmas cactus. "I didn't mean to startle you. It's so easy to startle people in here."

A woman stepped out from behind the cactus. The first thing I noticed about her were the two beautiful horns curling from the sides of her head. They were dark brown, speckled in some places by the dim white of unpolished bone. On the tip of the right horn was a thin satin ribbon in my favorite shade of light blue. Her loose-fitting linen dress was the same color.

I subtly checked the woman out as she stepped around the

huge cactus. She looked like a satyr with bat wings. She had a goat's head and she was covered in rich, reddish-brown fur. Her body was long and slender, her arms were short, and she had small, clawed hands. Large, leathery wings sprouted from her back, and a long, forked tail moved lazily behind her. She was uncannily beautiful. I was immediately glad that I'd worn a cute outfit today.

"Hi," I said, still a little stunned.

"Hi back," replied the woman. She grinned. "I'm Jersey. I don't think I've seen you in here before," she said.

"No, I—it's my first time," I stuttered. "Cleo," I added as an awkward afterthought.

"Your first time, huh? I'll go easy on you," the woman said. I felt my cheeks go warm at her innuendo. I prefer to move through the world with the assumption that everyone's hitting on me, but people don't usually make their interest so apparent. There's usually a bit more withholding, a bit more work on my end to draw them out. But this woman didn't seem like the type who needed to be drawn out.

"Can I help you find anything?" she asked. She didn't wait for me to answer before leading us farther into the store. When I heard the clattering noise again, I realized it was her hooves on the concrete floor. It was kind of a nice noise, soothing in the way that the *click-click-click* of high heels on hardwood could be soothing. I followed her without a second thought.

I knew Moonseed wasn't a large store, but it seemed to go on forever. With so many plants everywhere, I could never see all four walls at once. The air changed subtly as we walked, becoming a bit more humid, a bit cooler. The light grew a little darker. It made me think of something I learned a long time ago about the layers of rainforest: the tallest trees, the canopy, the understory, the undergrowth. I felt like I was following Jersey out of the canopy and into the understory. I realized I hadn't answered her question.

"I was looking for flowers," I said at last. "Do you sell flowers? Or is it just houseplants?" Jersey turned and smiled at me. She had horizontal pupils, and their uncanniness made her every glance feel extra mysterious, extra alluring.

"I have a little bit of everything," she said. Her hooves clicked against the cement floor as she led me to the back wall. This section of Moonseed was as brightly colored as the rest of the store was green. A large fridge lined the wall, and it was filled to the brim with cut flowers and bouquets in every color imaginable. I walked along the length of the fridge, admiring the peonies and roses, sunflowers and lilies, eucalyptus and ferns all cooling behind the glass.

"Are you shopping for anyone in particular? A friend?" Jersey asked, and then, with what I felt was a note of tension: "A partner?"

"No," I replied, "I'm just buying flowers for myself. I don't have a partner." I internally berated myself for delivering this information in such a blunt way. I took pride in my flirting abilities, and I couldn't come up with anything better than that? But my train of thought came to an abrupt stop when I saw a shimmer of pleasure in Jersey's strange eyes.

"In that case, I'd love to pick out a bouquet for you," she said. Her voice was low and soft. Her long eyelashes fluttered as she looked me up and down. I blushed immediately and profusely. My skin is dark enough that people don't always notice when I blush, but I knew Jersey saw it. I knew by the way her mouth quirked into a tiny, pleased smile. This only made me blush more. I nodded, not trusting myself to speak.

Jersey looked at the flowers, tapping a claw against her furry chin. I tried to pull myself together. I am, by any standards, excellent at flirting. I like being good at things, and flirting is something I'm very, very good at. So I was more than a little thrown off by this interaction with Jersey. I wasn't supposed to be stumbling around like this. I wasn't supposed to be stammering and blushing. I was supposed to be the one asking Jersey to choose a bouquet for me, because frankly that was a very sick move.

Jersey opened the fridge and reached behind some fresh-cut tulips. She pulled out a bouquet made up of dahlias and poppies and snapdragons and a few well-placed ferns. It was the ideal girl-carrying-a-bouquet-on-a-sunny-day bouquet. I was pleased and irritated all at once. I mentally shook myself. I looked up at Jersey and smiled in the way I always do when flirting, a smile that I think makes me look mysterious and coy and a little teasing.

"It's perfect," I said. I was about to add something when Jersey smiled back in the same teasing, inviting way. She was doing it better than me! My patented look! She even had the slightly lopsided grin down pat. I focused on not looking pissed.

"That's the bouquet I keep around for when pretty girls come into the store," she said. What the hell. It goes without saying that I blushed. My heart raced a little, although it did so against my will. I had to lock in.

"Do you get a lot of pretty girls coming through here?" I asked. Jersey shrugged.

"Only my favorite ones get the bouquet," she said. And what did I do? I giggled. I giggled and looked down at my shoes like a girl in a romance novel. This woman was two steps ahead of me at all times. I had to do something big.

"This is kind of forward," I said. "But would you happen to be free tonight? My friend is having a party at Screamin' Demon. You should come." Jersey blinked prettily at me, apparently a little surprised. That was good. I was finally getting the upper hand.

"I think that sounds nice," she said. That was when I realized I'd just asked this super hot woman to a party. I had kind of blacked out in my effort to win the interaction. But okay, cool, now I had a date for tonight. I still had some game.

I told Jersey the details as I followed her to the front of the shop. She rang me up.

"It was nice to meet you, Cleo," she said. She gave me a look that was a little coquettish and a little appraising.

"You too, beautiful." Nope. That was weird. That was super weird. I panicked and ran out of the store before she had a chance to respond. I felt a little calmer once I was back in the fresh air and out of that humid, plant-infested *Twilight Zone* episode.

I floated down the street in a daze. I was pretty sure something had taken control of my body in there. I don't claim to be the coolest person ever born, but that was crazy. I'd never been pushed so far off-balance. I was shaken up. I didn't like it. But then I thought about Jersey.

Jersey was the most beautiful woman I'd ever seen. Her strong, curled horns, her russet fur, her neatly folded wings. And her eyes, with their long eyelashes and otherworldly pupils that seemed to see things that I couldn't. And this beautiful woman had been flirting with *me*. Without my even needing to get the ball rolling. I sighed. The sun warmed my face. Maybe I needed to calm down a little. Maybe this wasn't so bad.

Step two of my beautiful day plan was to go to the bakery. The only thing more romantic than carrying around a bouquet of flowers was carrying around a bouquet of flowers and a loaf of bread. I headed to the bakery and tried to let myself get distracted by how nice the weather was. It was starting to get a little hotter than I wanted, but the occasional breeze solved that problem. I liked days when everyone was outside. This town was great for people-watching. Well, people- and cryptid-watching.

The city where Lucy and I used to live was always bustling, but people wouldn't really go out and walk around like this. Everyone was going from a primary location to a secondary location. But in the Creek, people wandered. A yeti and a bigfoot kissed on a street corner. A couple of older humans met up with a couple of older chupacabras to get lunch at the ramen shop. Some nightcrawlers were out window-shopping. It made the town feel more lived in, more connected.

The bell above the bakery door chimed as I walked in. It was lunchtime so there was a line, but I didn't mind waiting. I pushed my sunglasses onto my head and took a moment to appreciate the air-conditioning. I was basically back to normal when I heard a familiar voice behind me.

"Hey, beautiful," Jersey said. I whipped around and found her trying very hard not to laugh. I don't know what look was on my face, but a shadow of concern passed over hers. "Oh, I'm sorry. I'm not making fun of you, I promise. I thought it was cute," she said earnestly. I tried to smile in a way that looked natural.

"I've been known to be cute," I said. Finally, I managed to say something remotely cool. Maybe I was back. "Fancy meeting you here," I added. Okay, not quite back. But Jersey giggled.

"Fancy that," she said. "I think the universe is trying to tell us something." She winked and my mind went blank.

"Are you taking a lunch break or are you done for the day?" I asked when I could form words again. I would stick to the basics until I could trust myself to say normal things.

"I'm done for today," Jersey said. "My friend Swampy covers the afternoons."

"Oh, I know Swampy. He's a cool guy," I said. Jersey brightened.

"I guess everyone in this town knows each other," she said.

"Yeah, I guess so. That makes it kind of weird that we haven't met," I said, motioning between us. Jersey smiled.

"Like I said, it's the universe. Today's our day," she said. The line had moved enough that we were almost at the counter.

"In that case, we should probably hang out together," I ventured. Okay, I was warming up. I was going to turn this whole thing around.

"I think the universe probably wants us to go to the botanical garden," Jersey said.

"That's so funny, I was just thinking that the universe was telling me to spend the afternoon at the botanical garden with you," I said. Jersey's pupils widened and her ears fluttered in what I assumed was her version of blushing. I was so back.

I had my bouquet of flowers and my sourdough baguette and Jersey with me as we walked to the botanical garden. It was even more romantic than I could have hoped.

"So how come I haven't seen you at the bookstore?" I asked as we passed under the bower at the entrance to the garden.

"How come I haven't seen you at the plant shop?" Jersey asked, gently brushing a vine away from her face. She looked really pretty in the dappled light and shadow. We walked out from under the bower and into the sun, and I caught myself thinking that Jersey looked really pretty in the bright sunlight too. This woman was doing something to my head. I cleared my throat.

"I don't have much of a green thumb. Now I know that you're there, though, I'll try to stop by more often," I said. Jersey nodded thoughtfully.

"I hear a lot of people say that. It always makes me sad,

though. I can't imagine never having any plants around," she said. I didn't know what to do with her. I was finally getting back on my feet and now she didn't want to do flirty banter anymore? Frustration swelled in my chest, but I tamped it down. Maybe I should just lean into this. It was becoming clear that I couldn't anticipate Jersey, so maybe I should change tactics and just try to roll with it. I could be relaxed. Or, I could probably figure out how to be relaxed in the next few minutes. I glanced at Jersey.

"Maybe you can teach me how to take care of plants," I offered. Jersey looked up at me, her expression more sincere than I had seen it. I mentally patted myself on the back.

"I would love to," she said, and this started her on a long spiel about how plant care was a skill that needed practice like any other skill, and she had some recommendations for starter plants off the top of her head but she'd need to hear more about the light in my apartment before she steered me in any one direction, and had I ever tried growing herbs because those were pretty hard to kill and it always made Jersey feel so adult to cook with herbs that she'd grown herself.

I didn't say anything, just nodded and made sounds of affirmation when needed. And Jersey just kept going. She told me everything about all her favorite flowers and native plants and pollinators and on and on. At first, this made me a little uncomfortable. I didn't want Jersey to think I wasn't willing to have a back-and-forth with her, or that I needed her to do all the conversational heavy lifting. But then I remembered that I was being relaxed, so I released my anxiety and just listened while Jersey talked.

I didn't understand everything that she said, but what I did understand was really interesting. And it was just cool that she knew so much about plants. I wished I knew that much about anything. Jersey would occasionally interrupt herself to point out a flower she liked or explain which plants local butterfly species preferred. Her voice was low but clear and her slight lisp was very cute. By the end of the tour, I was really enjoying just hanging back and listening to her.

By the time we left the garden, I was dizzy with the smell of flowers and the sound of Jersey's voice. But I still wasn't tired of listening to her. She talked so excitedly, like she had been waiting her whole life to tell me everything she knew about plants. It was extremely endearing.

"Okay," I said when we left the garden, "now I think we should go to the bookstore. It's my turn to tell you about stuff."

Jersey laughed and followed me across the street to Bookwraith. It was about two o'clock and the weather was still holding strong. I kept expecting clouds to roll in, but if anything the sky was even bluer now than it was this morning.

At Bookwraith, there was a steady stream of customers coming in and out. Lucy was at the counter talking to CC about romance novels, Loveland and her daughter were browsing the memoirs, and Mason was restocking his zines. Light shone through the big front windows and Lucy had the front door open and the box fans going full blast to keep the store cool.

"Why are you here?" Lucy asked as soon as I came into the store. CC gave me a wave. As usual, he was looking extremely hot. I winked at him and he blushed dark green. Still got it. I turned to Lucy.

"You don't need to be rude," I said. Lucy rolled their eyes.

"You know what I mean," they said. I gestured to Jersey.

"My friend wanted to see the store. She hasn't been here before," I said. Lucy gave Jersey a once-over and I could tell they approved. Lucy and I both liked tall women, and Jersey was nothing if not tall.

"You run the plant store, right?" Lucy asked. Jersey nodded. "We aren't very good at plants, but that's a cute store," they said.

"We're going to be good at plants now," I said, "Jersey just gave me, like, a full botany class." Jersey's ears fluttered.

"I hope I didn't talk too much," she said.

"You didn't talk too much. I had a really nice time," I said sincerely. I rubbed her furry upper arm for emphasis. Jersey's pupils grew large and she smiled shyly. "Now tell me about what kind of books you like," I said, still looking into Jersey's eyes.

Jersey explained to me her love of Russian literature and I whisked her around the store, pointing out which books she would like or dislike, which authors I personally liked, which genre novels would be a little out of Jersey's comfort zone but in a fun way. It wasn't as long a tour as Jersey's tour of the botanical garden, and the conversation was more balanced, but it was nice to get to share some of my knowledge with Jersey after she had shared so much with me. Plus, I liked showing off the bookstore.

It was cute and Lucy and I had worked hard on it.

In the end, Jersey bought a sci-fi novella. She chose well. I was going to buy the book for her, but she insisted on paying herself. Lucy rang her up. While Lucy was doing that, I ran into the back to grab the quilt I'd left there at the end of last summer and two cans of sparkling water.

"Now leave and take advantage of this beautiful day or I'll make *you* stay here and work while *I* make eyes at a pretty girl," Lucy said to me.

"And how would Mothman feel about that?" I asked, pretending to be aghast.

"Mothman *is* the pretty girl," Lucy said, and grinned. I laughed and led Jersey out of the store.

"I think we should go to the park," I said when we were back outside. "I love going to the park."

"So do I," said Jersey. "The birch trees there are so beautiful this time of year." I smiled inwardly. We wandered back across the street to the park. I carried my bouquet and baguette and Jersey carried her book and the blanket and our drinks. Neither of us said much, but we kept perfect pace with each other. Occasionally the back of my hand would brush against Jersey's wing. I felt a bolt of electricity run through me whenever this happened.

"*Have* you been making eyes at me?" Jersey asked, breaking the silence.

"No, I'm stupid," I said without thinking. Jersey snorted. I tried to backpedal, realizing this was not exactly the smooth response that the situation warranted. "Sorry. I just mean, duh, I've been flirting with you. Why wouldn't I be flirting with you?" I elbowed Jersey lightly. Jersey elbowed me back. It was kind of starting to freak me out how much I liked hanging out with her.

When we got to the park, we found a shady spot under a tree to spread out the quilt and we both sat down. When I spread out our flowers and bread and drinks, I felt a cloud of butterflies in my chest. We'd accidentally set up the perfect romantic picnic. The sun was a little lower in the sky and a few bright clouds had rolled in. Still a beautiful day. I smiled at Jersey, but this time I wasn't trying to give her any particular kind of look. I was just smiling because I was happy to be here with her. She smiled back like she was thinking the same thing.

"I didn't even notice how tired I was until I sat down," I said as I pulled a hunk of bread from the loaf.

"Me neither," said Jersey, grabbing some bread for herself. "I guess being around you is pretty distracting." I opened our drinks and handed Jersey a can.

"Distracting how?" I asked, teasing. Jersey's long, thin tail was waving leisurely in the air behind her. It was almost hypnotic to watch. While I was paying attention to her tail, Jersey reached out and tucked one of my short locs behind my ear. It surprised me so much that I stopped messing with our food and just looked at her.

"Distracting because I'm so into you," she said. Her eyes flitted over me, her pupils thin in the sunlight. My heart did a little flip.

It's not that I was surprised to hear that she was into me, it's just that she said it so sincerely and without any apprehension. She wasn't doing a bit or playing a game. She was just talking to me.

"Honestly, it's kind of embarrassing how into you I am," Jersey continued, "I've only known you for a few hours." My heart did several more flips in quick succession.

"Every time I leave the house I hope I'm going to meet a hottie that I can have a crush on. I live to have a dumb little crush," I said. It felt a little weird being so honest with someone I just met, but I wanted to meet Jersey where she was at. She laughed.

"So do I," she said. "Today I have a dumb little crush on you." I smiled, and my smile was probably a little too big and too real, but I gave it to her anyway. Jersey ran the tip of her claw down the length of my arm. I shivered, my skin erupting in goosebumps. Right then, I would've sworn that Jersey and I were the only people in this park—in the world, even.

"Can I kiss you?" I asked. Jersey looked me straight in the eyes and nodded. She looked so happy. I took Jersey's face in my hands and leaned in. The kiss was warm and slow, almost lazy. I ran my hands through Jersey's fur and she ran her fingers along my jaw and we kissed without the heady chaos I often feel during a kiss—the need to move quickly from one thing to the next, the frenzy of two bodies suddenly meeting. We kissed like we were sharing something, like we were trying to get something right and had all the time in the world to figure it out. My whole body was relaxed, and when we finally broke apart I rolled lazily onto my back. Jersey giggled.

"Yeah," she said.

"Yeah," I echoed. Jersey lay next to me. We were both quiet; the kind of comfortable quiet that comes when nothing needs to be said. The sun stretched over us and warmed my face. I looked for clouds but found none. The sky was clear again.

The next thing I knew, I was opening my eyes to a dark sky and a firefly floating past my head. I sat up slowly, running a hand down my face. Jersey and I must have fallen asleep. I looked over to where Jersey lay on the old quilt, her head nestled in the crook of her arm, her tail curled up at her side. A firefly circled her head. She was even pretty when she was asleep.

With some reluctance, I shook Jersey's shoulder to wake her up. Jersey opened her eyes, her pupils wide in the dark, the fur on one side of her face stuck down. I grinned at the way she looked with her fur like that.

"What time is it?" Jersey asked as she rubbed her eyes. I checked my watch.

"Time for us to be fashionably late to the party," I said. Jersey was still lying down. She traced circles on my knee with a claw. A wave of goosebumps went through me every time she touched a claw to my skin.

"I guess we should go," Jersey said, still absently running a claw along my knee.

"I guess," I said, but she didn't move. Jersey looked up at me and must have seen the desire in my eyes. She smiled.

Then we were kissing again, more intensely than before but still with that sense of warmth. I put a hand on Jersey's neck and she let out a soft moan. Jersey snuck a hand up the back of my shirt and I shivered. Whenever I opened my eyes, I could only see fireflies.

We kissed for longer than before, until Jersey finally pulled away.

"I'm not having sex with you in this park," she said. I was woozy with kissing and didn't want to stop, but I agreed it was time to go.

We folded up the quilt and headed back into town. When I woke up this morning, I'd expected to have a simple day. Instead, I met Jersey, who was so hot and so smart and so funny, who knew everything a person could possibly know about plants, who loved to flirt and read classic Russian novels, who kissed me like I've never been kissed in my life. I thought that Jersey was right, that the universe had brought us together today.

I took Jersey's furry hand in mine and her ears fluttered. I didn't have to do anything else. This small gesture was enough.

On the way to the bar, we stopped at the plant shop to stash the quilt and kiss a little more. This time it was me who broke off, because I would never, ever make it to the bar if I kissed Jersey for even another second. We giggled as we came out of the plant shop and I took her hand again. The sky was summer-dark: that inky, luminous blue that comes after a clear June day. I glanced at Jersey and thought she looked really pretty in the dim light.

When we finally got to the bar, everyone was already there. Lucy and Mothman and CC and Romy and Mason and Swampy and Bridget. Mitch and Griffin and Theo and Flatwoods, and of course Sas and June. Outside, a group of kids and nightcrawlers skated by, whooping and yelling to one another.

All these wonderful friends in one place. The people I'd chosen to build a life with. The old friend I'd known forever and the new ones I already loved. The potential lover holding my hand in hers. A feeling washed over me then, something like joy and like melancholy and like nostalgia and like excitement. A looking forward and a looking back. A sudden ability to see my past and future all at once. And with this feeling came an indescribable sense of peace. I took a deep breath. Jersey squeezed my hand and we walked inside.

ACKNOWLEDGMENTS

Before I thank anyone else, I have to thank (profusely, unendingly, and likely to her great embarrassment) Jess Zimmerman. Jess is the best editor anyone could ask for, and I'm especially lucky to have her as a friend and mentor. I will always owe my career to Jess laughing at my stupid jokes and encouraging me to write about all the weird stuff I'm into. I'd also like to thank the rest of the team at Quirk, especially Kassie Andreadis, Jane Morley, and Paige Graff. Thank you to Wendy Stephens for the lovely illustrations and map (what a dream to have a map at the beginning of this book!). Thank you to my agent, Rebecca Podos, who loved Mothman right away and protected my vision for this project.

The biggest thank you to my friends! To my most trusted readers—Oliver Scialdone, Jay Loscar, Alex Juarez, Drew Broussard, and Calvin Kasulke—for giving me invaluable feedback and for seeing my stories so clearly. To Charlie Hunts and Madeline Burchard of Charlie's Queer Books, for giving me time and space in your store and for being the best cheerleaders. To Emma, Clara, Lauren, Harrison, Maggie, Bianca, and Alana, for being the best friends in the world. To my family for always, always supporting and loving me. And to my siblings, Rosie and Seamus, two of my favorite people in the world, who gave me so much while I was writing this book and who give me so much always.

McKAYLA COYLE (they/them) is a lesbian writer from Alaska currently living in Washington. They're the author of *Goblin Mode: How to Get Cozy, Embrace Imperfection, and Thrive in the Muck* and the publishing coordinator for Literary Hub, and they hold an MFA in fiction from the New School. In their free time they read a lot of fantasy novels and make a lot of jam.

MOTHMAN IS MY ~~BOYFRIEND~~ DADDY

WANT TO GO UNDER THE COVERS WITH YOUR FAVORITE CRYPTIDS?

Welcome to Cryptid Creek . . . after dark!
For true cryptid fans only, the digital edition of *Mothman Is My Boyfriend* includes three kinky bonus stories. Available wherever e-pubs are sold.